Books in the American Dog series:

Brave

Chestnut

Star

AMERICAN DOG
★ POPPY ★

BY JENNIFER LI SHOTZ

HOUGHTON MIFFLIN HARCOURT
BOSTON   NEW YORK

Produced by Alloy Entertainment

30 Hudson Yards
New York, NY 10001

The text was set in Adobe Caslon Pro.

Library of Congress Cataloging in Publication Data
Names: Shotz, Jennifer Li, author.
Title: Poppy / by Jennifer Li Shotz.
Description: Boston ; New York : Houghton Mifflin Harcourt, [2020] | Series: American dog | Summary: With the help of a very special pit bull puppy, twelve-year-old Hannah adjusts to moving from Michigan to California and makes friends, despite the birthmark that makes her self-conscious.
Identifiers: LCCN 2019016729 (print) | LCCN 2019019320 (ebook) | ISBN 9780358108627 (E-book)
Subjects: | CYAC: Moving, Household—Fiction. | Birthmarks—Fiction. | Pit bull terriers—Fiction. | Dogs—Fiction. | Friendship—Fiction. | Family life—California—Fiction. | California, Southern—Fiction.
Classification: LCC PZ7.1.S51784 (ebook) | LCC PZ7.1.S51784 Pop 2020 (print) | DDC [Fic]—dc23
LC record available at https://lccn.loc.gov/2019016729

ISBN: 978-0-358-10869-6 paper over board
ISBN: 978-0-358-10873-3 paperback

Manufactured in the United States of America
DOC 10 9 8 7 6 5 4 3 2 1
4500793142

To anyone who has ever felt a little different.

★ CHAPTER 1 ★

Hannah pretended to study the rows of bagged salad mix and baby spinach as another shopper pushed a cart past her. She felt more than saw the man's eyes on her as he walked by. She kept the right side of her face turned away, her long, straight brown hair falling across her cheek like a curtain. She wished her mom would hurry up and finish picking out produce. She wanted to be back in her room, away from all the eyes turned in her direction.

It wasn't that people hadn't stared at Hannah in Michigan—they had. But her friends and teachers never treated her any differently because of the blotchy, reddish-purple birthmark that covered almost half of her face. Her friends had made it easier to ignore the sneaked glances and curious stares of strangers. But ever since her family had moved to California, the stares felt heavy and uncomfortable.

"Hannah, come see these avocados!" her mom exclaimed.

"We had avocados in Michigan," Hannah muttered to the spinach.

"Yes, but not like these." Her mom wrapped an arm around her shoulders and steered Hannah over to a pyramid of fruit. "We'll make guacamole. You love guacamole. It'll be even better because these are local!"

Her mom's voice had skipped into its too-cheerful tone, which had happened a lot since they'd moved to Deerwood. She kept saying things like *This is just like your favorite thing, only better!*

Except everything was worse here.

Hannah used to love making guacamole with her best friend, Linnea. They'd mash a big bowl of it, then sit on the living room floor with a bag of those tortilla chips in the shape of tiny little scoops. They'd eat the whole bowl while they watched movies. Local avocados wouldn't make up for her friend—for *all* of her friends—being so far away.

The scene her mom was making over the avocados was drawing even more stares.

"Okay, fine," Hannah said. "Can we just go?"

Hannah had wanted to stay home and hide with a book among the huge trees behind their house, away from the crying twins. But as soon as her dad returned from dropping her little sister off at soccer camp and the twins had gone down for their nap, her mom had decided they needed mother-daughter bonding time. Being dragged across town just to go to Safeway for groceries wasn't Hannah's idea of bonding, even with her mom's promise that they could stop for ice cream on the boardwalk on the way home.

Her mom's excitement slipped into a frown. But before she could say anything to Hannah about her attitude, another woman approached them.

"Oh, hi there!" The woman sounded extra friendly, just like everyone else who made a point of introducing themselves to the new family in town. "You live in the yellow ranch house on Cedar Drive, right?"

"That's us." Hannah's mom returned the woman's warm smile.

"I'm Dana Lin," she said. "We live in the blue two-story around the corner."

"I wasn't expecting to meet any of our neighbors in the produce aisle," Hannah's mom said.

Mrs. Lin laughed. "Well, it's not a farmers' market day."

"I'm Lila Carson," Hannah's mom said. "This is my daughter Hannah — my oldest."

"Hi!" Hannah said, forcing herself to sound as perky and nice as Mrs. Lin had. Her parents had always told her that being polite was the first step to helping people look past her birthmark.

Mrs. Lin turned toward Hannah for the first time, and

her smile fell into a look of surprise mixed with a little bit of pity—and a lot of questions. Like most adults, she recovered quickly. "It's so nice to meet you, Hannah. What grade are you in?"

"I'll be starting sixth," Hannah said.

"That's my daughter's grade." She took her eyes off Hannah's face to scan the produce section. "Sophia, come over here!"

A girl who'd been standing by the strawberries, typing on her phone, walked toward them without glancing up. She was slightly taller than Hannah, with long, thick black hair tied back in a loose ponytail. Her skin was clear and tan from the summer sun, with a dusting of tiny freckles across her nose.

"Sophia, these are our new neighbors," Mrs. Lin said. "Hannah will be in your class this year."

Sophia slowly looked up from her phone, her lips curving into a smile as she started to say hello. But when her gaze landed on Hannah, she froze, her mouth slightly open.

Heat crept up Hannah's face as Sophia stared. She knew that blushing only made her birthmark worse. Now her whole face was probably blotchy, instead of just the ragged patch that looked like a stain spreading from her chin to her eyebrow.

Hannah wished she could hide behind the avocados.

She didn't want to have to explain that she had been born with it and it would never go away. She didn't want to have to see how long it would take this girl with perfect skin to get used to looking at her — let alone get to know her. She wasn't sure if Sophia would even try.

She knew she should ask Sophia about school or at least say it was nice to meet her. But her tongue lay like a fat marshmallow in her mouth.

"We should all get together back in the neighborhood," Mrs. Lin said a little too brightly. "How old are your other kids?"

"Jenny is eight. And my twin boys are eighteen months."

"Wow, you have your hands full! Sophia has a younger sister too, so it'll be perfect."

"Sounds great," Hannah's mom said. "Hannah hasn't really met anyone since we moved here."

Embarrassment flared across Hannah's cheeks again. She tried to hide behind her hair, but it was too late. Sophia was back on her phone. She was probably telling all the other kids in their class about the new girl with the stained face and no friends.

"Why don't you all come over for brunch on Saturday?" Hannah's mom said.

Hannah flashed her a look, but her mom didn't notice.

"We'd love to," Mrs. Lin said.

★ ★ ★

"This is exciting," Hannah's mom said after Sophia and Mrs. Lin had headed toward the bread aisle. "You haven't had a playdate since we moved here."

"Mom, no one has playdates anymore," Hannah grumbled. She dreaded a whole morning of Sophia staring at her over pancakes.

"You know what I mean." Her mom sighed. "You've hardly left the house all summer."

"Well, on the upside, I haven't gotten a single sunburn this year."

Hannah thought she'd get a lecture on putting herself out in the world, but her mom was distracted by a display of tortillas. The avocados must have inspired her to make tacos for dinner. Normally, Hannah would have been excited about taco night, but just then she heard Sophia and her mom talking down the next aisle.

"It's hard to be the new kid in town," Mrs. Lin said. "You can still see your friends later in the afternoon."

"But what's wrong with her face?" Sophia asked.

Her mom shushed her. "Don't be rude."

Their voices faded as they walked away. Tears stung Hannah's eyes. The noises of the grocery store rose and fell around her—cash registers dinged and shopping carts clanged together. But even surrounded by the steady hum and buzz of the store, she felt lonely—separate from everyone around her, trapped behind the stain on her face.

Hannah missed her friends. They knew that the birthmark was just one small part of who she really was.

"Can we please go?" she asked quietly.

Her mom tossed a package of tortillas into the cart and turned to look at her. Hannah didn't think she'd heard what Sophia said, but her mom saw the tears in her eyes. "Oh, honey. It always takes time to make new friends."

"Jenny already has friends," Hannah said, thinking about how her younger sister had it so easy.

"It's different when you're little." Her mom brushed the hair back from Hannah's birthmark. "You'll see. Once people get to know you, it'll be even better than before."

Hannah pulled away from her mom. It was easy for her parents to say how great everything would be here. It had been their decision to move to some little town, a random dot dropped along the map of the California coastline. And they didn't have people constantly asking what was wrong with them.

★ CHAPTER 2 ★

Hannah sat on the giant Adirondack chair on the front porch, her legs tucked under her. Between texts to Linnea and rounds of *Candy Crush,* she glanced up and down the street. She hoped to spot a deer or a fox so she could send Linnea a picture of her new neighbors.

Hannah had to admit it was pretty out here, even if there was nothing to do. When the wind blew in the right direction, she caught the clean, salty smell of the ocean, and not far from town there were redwood trees so huge her whole family could hold hands and still not wrap their arms all the way around the trunks. And there was a ton of wildlife —so much more than the squirrels and raccoons they had in Michigan. Sometimes Hannah heard coyotes howling at night, and she'd even seen a bald eagle perched in the big fir tree across the street.

But today there was no wildlife in sight, just her

next-door neighbor, Mrs. Gilly, slowly making her way down her driveway.

Mrs. Gilly's walker glinted silver in the sunlight. According to Hannah's mom, she had just had hip surgery, which explained why Hannah hadn't seen her around much. She was a slight woman, older than Hannah's parents. Her gray-streaked hair was knotted in a loose bun. She wore a light khaki vest with lots of small pockets, like a safari guide or a fisherman, and she had a leash looped around one wrist.

At the other end of the leash was a thick-chested, stocky dog with muscular legs. The pup wore a pale pink harness and blue collar. She had a blocky head, short light brown fur with patches of white, and one big spot over her eye and down the side of her face. She practically pranced down the driveway, and when she gazed up at Mrs. Gilly with her tongue hanging out, it looked like she was smiling. As the dog's tail whipped back and forth, she seemed to be the happiest dog in the world.

Hannah had never had a dog of her own and had never really paid much attention to them, but she had to admit that this one was pretty cute. Her smile was simply irresistible, and something about her bright personality reminded Hannah of the California sunshine.

The dog stretched out her front legs and lowered her burly chest to the ground in a playful bow, then leaped up again. Mrs. Gilly's walker had tennis balls attached to the bottom of the front legs to help her glide around easily, but the dog seemed to think they were her toys. She dove for the tennis balls, tipping her head sideways and trying to gnaw on one of them.

"Poppy, no!" Mrs. Gilly cried. "Sit."

The dog sat. But a second later she popped up and pounced on the ball again, nearly yanking Mrs. Gilly and her walker over. Without thinking, Hannah jumped out of her chair and ran across the yard. She snatched up the half-deflated soccer ball Jenny had left in the dry grass and skidded to a stop a few feet from the dog.

"Hey, Poppy!" Hannah sang in a friendly voice. The dog looked her way, the tips of her floppy ears dancing forward. Hannah rolled the soccer ball to her, and the dog pounced on it. Hannah held her breath, hoping Poppy wouldn't pull Mrs. Gilly too hard and make her lose her balance. She didn't want to make things worse.

Poppy wrestled the soccer ball with her front paws, then managed to pick it up between her teeth, even though it was as big as her head. The ball jutted out of her mouth, and she wagged her tail so hard that her whole body wriggled back and forth. She looked at Hannah as if thanking her for the toy. The dog was bursting with such happiness, Hannah couldn't help but laugh out loud.

"That was good thinking," Mrs. Gilly said. "Would you mind helping me fix her leash?"

"Sure thing," Hannah said. Her cheeks flushed hot again, but this time it wasn't from embarrassment. This time it was something else—the funny feeling she got in her chest when she helped her mom with one of the twins or managed to cheer up a grumpy Jenny. It was a small swell of satisfaction.

"Do you see the little loop on the front of her harness?" Mrs. Gilly asked. Hannah nodded. "If you clip the leash to that, she can't pull so hard. I should have done it that way, but I'm still getting used to this walker."

"Oh, no problem!" Hannah said. She leaned down toward the dog, and Poppy dropped the ball to lick her face. Hannah laughed—trying to dodge the dog's huge, slobbery tongue—reclipped the leash, and stood up again. Poppy was watching her closely, but it wasn't anything like the long, awkward stares Hannah got from new people she met.

Poppy was looking at her as if she wanted to be friends.

"Thank you," Mrs. Gilly said to Hannah. She dipped her fingers into one of her many vest pockets, pulled out a treat, and held it out to the dog. Hannah expected Poppy to snatch it from Mrs. Gilly's fingers and gobble it down, but Poppy took it gently between her teeth and eased it into her mouth as if she were savoring it.

"She seems like a really good dog," Hannah said. She ran her fingers over the patch of brown fur that covered half of Poppy's face . . . almost like a birthmark. Her fur was smooth and velvety. Poppy finished her treat and licked Hannah's hand.

"She is," Mrs. Gilly said, giving Poppy a loving but exasperated look. "She just doesn't know what to do with all her energy. She's only six months old."

"I could help you walk her," Hannah blurted out before she even realized what she was saying. "I mean—if that's all right with you." She'd never actually walked a dog, but there was something about Poppy that made Hannah want to play with her.

"Are you sure?" Mrs. Gilly asked.

Hannah nodded, saying, "I'll be right back," as much to Poppy as to her neighbor.

She ran to her house, flung open the front door, and grabbed her Detroit Tigers baseball cap, pulling it low over her face. She put on sunblock every morning, but her face burned easily. "Mom, I'm going for a walk!" she called.

Her mom was in the kitchen, strapping Noah and Logan into their highchairs. She didn't even turn around, and Hannah was back out the door before her mom could ask any questions. When Hannah returned, Poppy bounced on her front paws as if Hannah were her favorite person in the world.

Hannah grinned at the dog. "I told you I'd be right back."

"I'm so glad. Here, take this." Mrs. Gilly held out the leash to Hannah. Imitating the way Mrs. Gilly had held it, Hannah put her hand through the loop and grabbed onto the thick, woven rope farther down. The three of them started down the driveway. Poppy was excited to be on the move and clearly had some pent-up energy. Even though the harness kept her from pulling too hard, her leash was taut. Hannah had to lean back a little to slow Poppy down to Mrs. Gilly's pace.

Poppy was curious about everything. Her tail slowed to a thoughtful sway as her nose explored a particularly interesting tree trunk or a patch of weeds. When she was done sniffing, she glanced at Hannah before forging ahead, her tail picking up speed.

"How come I've never seen you out walking with Poppy?" Hannah said to Mrs. Gilly.

"I had to board her while I recovered from surgery," the older lady said. "But I missed her so much, I brought her home as soon as I could." Mrs. Gilly looked down at her dog with a bit of sadness in her eyes. "Maybe too soon," she added softly, almost as if she didn't want Poppy or Hannah to hear.

They walked in silence for a few minutes. Mrs. Gilly fell a few steps behind, and Hannah led Poppy back toward her.

They stopped in the shade of a tree at the edge of a neighbor's yard, and Mrs. Gilly leaned against her walker. Poppy flopped down and rolled onto her side in the cool dirt, content and relaxed. Hannah sat on the ground next to her and stroked her silky fur.

"How do you like it here so far?" Mrs. Gilly asked once she'd caught her breath.

Hannah shrugged. "It's okay, I guess."

"New places always take some getting used to—I felt that way when I moved here," Mrs. Gilly said. "Have you made any friends yet?"

Hannah frowned and shook her head, her face turned away. Poppy stopped chewing on the stick she'd found. She tilted her head to the side, as if she were listening in on their conversation. Hannah scratched the dog's tummy.

"You and Poppy, I guess . . ." Hannah said before trailing off.

"Well, that's sweet, dear. I bet when school starts, you'll make lots of friends your own age," Mrs. Gilly said. "I think you're probably in the same grade as my granddaughter, and she has zoodles of friends."

"I'm not so sure." Hannah lifted her chin and met Mrs. Gilly's eyes, giving her a good look at her birthmark. Was it possible she hadn't noticed it?

Mrs. Gilly looked right into Hannah's face without

flinching. She gave a knowing nod. "Poppy knows what it's like to be misunderstood."

"What do you mean?" Hannah asked.

"People think she's a bad dog just because she's a pit bull. And people think pit bulls are mean."

"Because of what she looks like?" Hannah asked, confused. Poppy had the biggest grin and hadn't stopped wagging her tail for a second since she'd left the house. Even now, her tail brushed back and forth against the ground. "But she's so friendly."

"She is. But a lot of people won't even give her a chance because of the way she looks," Mrs. Gilly said.

Hannah tried to see Poppy the way other people might. She took in the dog's square jaw and strong muscles, but those paled in comparison to her bright, sparkling eyes and kind face. Poppy's tongue dangled out of her mouth as she looked up at Hannah and blinked a couple of times.

"Well, I think she's a special dog," Hannah said.

Mrs. Gilly turned to Hannah. For the first time since she'd moved to California, Hannah felt that someone was looking at *her*, and not at her birthmark.

"She *is* special," Mrs. Gilly said. "And it takes a special kind of person to sense the goodness in Poppy and not just see her as a scary dog."

Mrs. Gilly's words went straight to Hannah's heart.

Poppy put her head down on Hannah's leg, gazing up at her with her soft brown eyes. As Hannah looked down at the dog, she realized that Poppy would never understand why people were scared of her; she only wanted people to like her. Hannah scratched Poppy behind the ear—right by the brown patch of fur that spread across half of her face.

★ CHAPTER 3 ★

Hannah and her mom spent Saturday morning making fresh doughnuts, fruit salad, and a frittata for brunch. It was fun being in the kitchen together. Between unpacking, starting a big project for a new client, and caring for the twins, her mom had been so busy since they'd moved that they'd barely had time to boil pasta for dinner.

While they waited for the doughnuts to cool, Hannah shook a bottle of rainbow sprinkles, a makeshift rattle for Noah. Her baby brother was mesmerized by the colors, and it kept him from trying to grab the bowls of powdered sugar and maple icing.

"Where did you go yesterday afternoon?" her mom asked. "I heard you race out the door."

"Just for a walk," Hannah said. "I met Mrs. Gilly's dog! Mrs. Gilly was having trouble balancing her walker and the leash."

"Mrs. Gilly has a dog?"

"Her name is Poppy." Hannah dipped a doughnut in the powdered sugar and put it on a platter. "She has these cute brown patches and she's always wagging her tail."

"She sounds happy," her mom said, drizzling icing on half a dozen doughnuts in a zigzag pattern.

"She is. And she's really friendly." Hannah raised her voice to be heard over Noah banging the bottle of sprinkles on the tray of his highchair. She hoped she'd remembered to screw the lid on extra tight.

"Well, I'm glad you got outside, honey." Her mom wiped her hands on a dishtowel, then wiped a bit of powdered sugar from Hannah's cheek. "And now you look like you've been in the snow."

"Hmm . . . snow, huh?" Hannah said, as if she were struggling to recall a distant memory. "I vaguely remember that from my old life."

"Very funny," her mom replied with an ever-so-slight eye roll. "Now go get changed. Sophia will be here soon for your playdate."

"*Mom*—" Hannah groaned. "Please stop calling it that."

"You know what I mean."

Hannah headed to her room and stopped in front of the mirror. Her blue T-shirt was dusted with powdery white sugar. Powdery like snow. Just the thought of it made her wish for her old friends, who wouldn't care what was on her face—sugar or otherwise.

Hannah sighed. If only she could wear this shirt, maybe Sophia would stare at her messy clothes instead of her birthmark. She changed into her favorite pink top and jean shorts and brushed out her hair. When she was done, she sent a selfie to Linnea. A few seconds later Linnea texted back a string of emojis to tell her she looked great. Hannah smiled. Maybe it would be different today—maybe Sophia was just taken by surprise at the supermarket. Maybe today she'd be used to the birthmark.

The doorbell rang. Hannah took a deep breath and opened her bedroom door. She took one step into the hall and was almost run over by Sophia's little sister and Jenny whipping past. Her mom's voice chased after them. "Five minutes, girls. Then it's time to eat! You can play more after brunch."

Her heart pounding in her chest, Hannah headed for the living room. She had barely crossed the threshold when her dad popped Logan into her arms. "Can you hang on to your brother for a second?" he asked, his voice strained. "I need to change Noah." He didn't give Hannah much choice as he turned away and disappeared into the twins' bedroom, leaving her holding a chunky, squirming baby.

Hannah looked down at her baby brother's face as he

studied her with his serious blue eyes. Somehow he had powdered sugar on his forehead, even though he hadn't been in the kitchen when they'd been making brunch. Before she could wipe it off, Logan dropped his head forward onto her shoulder and let out a contented squeal. So much for her clean shirt.

Hannah sighed and rubbed her cheek against his downy soft head. She loved the twins, but they needed constant attention. She couldn't help it—sometimes she felt like she was just another pair of arms to hold them, feed them, and clean up after them. She thought back to the days when her family used to do fun things in the summer—wade in the lake on hot days or hop in the car after dinner to drive to their favorite ice cream stand. They'd all get double scoops, even though Jenny could never finish hers. But then the twins came along and changed everything.

Now it was too hard to pile everyone into the minivan for a spur-of-the-moment family outing. Besides, with two new babies, her dad's promotion at the solar panel company—which was why they'd moved across the country—and her mom's booming graphic design business, Hannah's parents never had free time to do anything fun. They could barely juggle it all. Jenny was too little to help out, but Hannah felt as if she had twice as many chores since they moved. Some days she felt like a built-in babysitter.

Logan raised his head and giggled at her. Hannah kissed his forehead, which tasted faintly sweet from the last of the powdered sugar. She carried him through the house, toward the sound of her mom and Mrs. Lin chatting like old friends. She didn't hear any other voices. For a second Hannah thought that maybe Sophia hadn't come over after all, though she wasn't sure if that made her feel relieved or disappointed. But when Hannah reached the sunny dining room, Sophia was there, standing behind her parents and looking down at her phone.

"Hi, honey," Hannah's mom said, taking Logan from her, and Mrs. Lin instantly began to coo and make big-eyed faces at him. This was Hannah's chance. If they forgot all about her, she could just slip back to her room.

"Sophia, Hannah—you remember each other from the grocery store?" Mrs. Lin said.

Hannah nodded. How could she forget? Barely raising her eyes, Sophia flashed a smile in Hannah's direction. Hannah knew it wasn't a real smile. Her mouth felt dry, but she felt like she should say something. Before a single word could come out, the two younger girls came thundering into the room.

"Is it time to eat yet?" Jenny asked. "We're so hungry."

"We're starving!" Sophia's little sister echoed. She looked like a miniature Sophia, with the same black hair and light freckles across her nose.

"We'd better feed you, then." Hannah's mom smiled and ushered the girls to the table.

Mrs. Lin admired the carefully set table and heaping platters of food. "Everything looks amazing."

"Hannah helped me make it," her mom said.

"I'm so impressed," Mrs. Lin said to Hannah. "Sophia can barely manage to make herself a peanut butter and jelly sandwich."

Hannah thought she saw something flicker across Sophia's downturned face, but she couldn't be sure.

"That's not true," Sophia muttered.

Everyone but Sophia sat down, leaving one empty seat between Hannah and Mrs. Lin. Sophia took the empty spot, and Hannah cringed. Somehow Sophia had wound up sitting to her right—the same side as her birthmark. Hannah shifted in her chair and shook her head gently, swinging her loose hair so it fell across her cheek.

Sophia didn't look at Hannah as they passed around the platter of doughnuts and the giant bowl of cut fruit. She kept her eyes cast down on her plate—which at least meant that she wasn't staring at Hannah's face.

The adults talked about the twins and asked Jenny about soccer camp. Hannah thought maybe they would forget about her and Sophia, but no such luck. It wasn't long before her dad noticed that neither one of them had said anything.

"So, Sophia, have you been having a good summer?" he asked.

Much to Hannah's surprise, Sophia's face lit up.

"We got a puppy," she gushed. "His name is Louie. He's a Mini Goldendoodle, and he's perfect. We did a couple of one-on-one sessions with a trainer, and she *loved* him. We're about to start a group training class."

Sophia pulled up a few videos on her phone and passed it around. Hannah's mom held it out to the twins, who shouted "Puppy!" in unison, making everyone laugh.

When the phone reached Hannah, she couldn't help but glance at the videos. They were of Louie learning how to sit, stay, and walk like a little gentleman on his leash. Hannah kept thinking of the way Poppy had yanked her down the street the day before, and she had to stop herself from making a face.

She suddenly understood why people misjudged dogs like Poppy, who were big and strong and playful compared with gentle little fluffballs like Louie, who had perfect manners. Even Hannah couldn't deny it: Sophia's puppy was adorable. But she also thought Poppy was the sweetest and friendliest dog she'd ever met, and she wished she had videos of Poppy to show off too. Sophia wasn't the only one who'd been spending time with a cute dog.

"And how has your summer been so far, Hannah?" Sophia's dad asked. "I bet you've been down at the beach a lot."

Hannah swallowed her mouthful of eggs and smiled politely. "A little bit." The truth was, they'd spent one afternoon walking down to the beach when they'd first moved in — it was less than a mile away — but her parents hadn't had much time to take her since then, and she didn't want to go alone.

"There are always kids at the beach, surfing," Sophia's dad went on. "You should join them."

Out of the corner of her eye, Hannah saw Sophia shift uncomfortably in her chair.

"Sophia, aren't you and your friends headed down this afternoon?" Mrs. Lin asked. "You could introduce Hannah to everyone."

Hannah tried not to notice when Sophia's gaze flicked to her, then to her mom. "I don't think we're going," she said.

"You aren't?" Mrs. Lin gave her daughter a confused look. "But you're at the beach every day—"

"Taylor has a thing she has to do for her mom . . ."

The table went quiet. It was obvious that Sophia was lying.

"It's okay," Hannah blurted out. "I have stuff to do. Plus, I don't even know how to surf." That part was true. She'd gone paddleboarding with her friends at the lake last summer, but she'd been in the ocean only a couple of times, and the big waves had scared her. She definitely didn't feel like embarrassing herself in front of Sophia and her friends. Still, she couldn't help feeling hurt that Sophia didn't even want her to meet them.

Thankfully, the conversation turned to her dad's new job, and soon there were only scraps of food left on the plates. Hannah's mom suggested that they all move to the back patio for lemonade. Everyone stood up, fake groaning and patting their stomachs and complimenting Hannah and her mom on the food. Sophia's little sister and Jenny shot off down the hall to Jenny's room. Sophia asked where the bathroom was, and Hannah's mom pointed after them.

"I'll clear the table, Mom," Hannah said.

Her mom studied her for a second and brushed her hand across Hannah's cheek. "Just do a little, then come join us, okay?"

Hannah nodded. As she stacked the dishes, she noticed that Sophia had left her phone next to her plate. She tried to ignore it, but when she came back to collect the juice glasses, the phone buzzed. Hannah couldn't resist taking a peek.

A text from Taylor lit up on the home screen. *The waves are PERFECT. When can you get here?*

Hannah's stomach did a little loop. She told herself it was fine—it's not like she wanted to hang out with Sophia anyway. Hannah left the phone and the rest of the dishes on the table and went out to the patio. The summer weather hit her like a brick wall. It was hotter than usual, and sweat trickled down her neck. Swimming in the ocean would probably feel good on a day like this. She cringed at the thought, knowing that she'd never be invited to the beach if Sophia had anything to do with it.

The parents had claimed the wraparound wicker sofa on one side of the deck, and the twins played on a blanket at their feet. That left the two lounge chairs on the other side for Hannah and Sophia. Hannah sat down, wishing she could be anywhere else right now.

Sophia came outside and pulled her thick black hair into a ponytail. Hannah wished she could do the same, but she wasn't ready to leave her birthmark uncovered in front of all these new people. She had felt so different with Mrs. Gilly and Poppy. With them she could just be herself.

Sophia sank into the empty lounge chair without so

much as a glance in Hannah's direction and went right back to texting her friends.

Suddenly a gray rabbit raced across the backyard, making a beeline toward the woods, followed by a big brown and white dog.

It was Poppy! Somehow she'd escaped.

Sophia dropped her phone in a panic. "It's a killer dog!" she shrieked, hugging her knees to her chest. "Oh my God, it's coming after us."

"No she's not!" Hannah said as she hopped up and bounded down the porch steps. "That's just our neighbor's dog."

Hannah raced after the puppy and called to her. "Here, Poppy!"

At the sound of her name, Poppy left the rabbit alone and ran over to Hannah, the tips of her ears bouncing. She greeted Hannah with a huge, panting grin, her tongue lolling out of her mouth.

"Hey, remember me?" Hannah knelt and scratched the top of the dog's big, solid head. Poppy leaned into her hand as if they were old friends. "What are you doing out here all by yourself?" Hannah looked around, but she didn't see Mrs. Gilly. Poppy must have gotten outside on her own and run off.

"Are you crazy?" Sophia called from the porch. "That's a pit bull, and she's going to eat you."

With a grimace, Hannah realized that these were the first words Sophia had ever said to her directly.

Hannah turned and glared at her. "No, actually she's not. Pit bulls are misunderstood, and Poppy is the sweetest."

"That's what people always say before they get eaten," Sophia said. She'd gotten over her fear long enough to rescue her phone from the ground. She pulled her legs up on her chair again, as if she were floating in shark-infested waters. Poppy just kept wagging her tail—Hannah was glad she had no idea what mean things Sophia was saying about her.

Hannah ignored Sophia's comment and turned to her parents. Her dad had scooped the twins onto his lap even as Logan's little hands stretched toward the dog.

"Wow, Hannah, that's quite a big puppy Mrs. Gilly has—" her dad said.

"Puppy!" The boys giggled.

"Why don't you take her back home before she gets into more trouble?" her dad finished.

Part of Hannah wanted Poppy to stay—at least so she'd have a friend at this boring brunch. But she knew her dad was right, and she was a little worried that the grownups might be scared of Poppy, too.

"Sure thing, Dad," Hannah said, standing up, her hand tight around the dog's collar.

"Thank you, sweetie," her mom said. "But come right back before the Lins leave. And tell Mrs. Gilly we say hello."

"I will," Hannah promised. She felt less anxious with the dog by her side. Hannah didn't especially want to come back after she dropped Poppy off, but at least she could make a brief escape. Maybe Poppy had somehow magically read her mind and run into the yard to rescue her. Even though it was a silly idea, the thought made Hannah smile. Unlike Sophia, Poppy actually wanted to spend time with her.

Hannah turned to face Sophia and, with her free hand, tucked her hair behind her right ear. "I can't go to the beach today anyway. I promised I'd help watch Poppy."

Hannah walked away without waiting for Sophia's reaction. Poppy trotted alongside her. They were both grinning from ear to ear.

★ CHAPTER 4 ★

While she waited for Mrs. Gilly to answer the door, Hannah held Poppy's collar to keep her from running off again. She didn't mind waiting. The longer it took for her to return Poppy, the less time she'd have to spend with Sophia.

Hannah was fuming. Who was that girl anyway? She couldn't believe the things Sophia had said about Poppy, who only wanted to play. Even now, the dog was tugging and wriggling in Hannah's grip, trying to pounce on a leaf blowing across the porch.

Finally the front door swung open.

Mrs. Gilly had her phone pressed to her ear. "It's Poppy," she said. "She's back!" She waved Hannah inside. "I know . . . thank goodness. I'll call you later."

She hung up her cell phone and closed the door behind them. Once it was firmly shut, she leaned over to rub Poppy's ears. "There you are! Where did you run off to?"

Poppy danced around her, tail wagging, as if Mrs. Gilly had been the one who'd run away.

"She was chasing a rabbit through my yard," Hannah said. She didn't want Poppy to get in too much trouble, so she added, "She came right to me when I called her."

"She must really like you," Mrs. Gilly said. Hannah felt honored, as if Poppy had chosen her. The feeling was mutual.

As soon as Mrs. Gilly stopped petting her, the dog dashed into the kitchen. Hannah could hear her slurping noisily at her water bowl, thirsty from her adventure.

"I was so worried about her. I opened the door to get the newspaper, and she just zipped out. I couldn't exactly chase after her." Mrs. Gilly gestured at her walker, frowning at it in frustration.

"She's really fast," Hannah said. "But she didn't try to get away again when I brought her home."

"Thank goodness. I was just calling my friend to come help me find her, but she lives all the way across town."

"You can always call me if you need help," Hannah offered. "Since we're right next door." She made the offer without thinking. In Michigan, she and her family were always helping their neighbors, and vice versa—wasn't that what neighbors did? But once she said it, Hannah realized how much she meant it. She'd be happy to help with Poppy anytime. Hannah couldn't quite describe it, but even though they'd just met, Poppy felt like more than just a dog—she felt like a friend.

Mrs. Gilly led Hannah from the foyer to the living room. Sun beamed through the windows onto a big couch with plump cushions. A small tuft of stuffing poked out of one pillow from a hole that looked suspiciously like Poppy had chewed it. The walls were lined with bookshelves. Books, candles, framed photos, and hand-carved wooden animals were crammed onto the highest shelves, while the lower, dog-level shelves were bare.

"I really can't thank you enough, Hannah." Mrs. Gilly eased herself into an armchair and set her walker aside. "Poppy doesn't always listen to everyone, you know."

Hannah shrugged, but there was that little flush of happiness and pride in her chest again. "She's a good dog."

Mrs. Gilly gestured for Hannah to make herself at home. Hannah sank into the couch, which was so cozy it seemed to be hugging her. Little drifts of Poppy's brown fur clung to the soft beige fabric. Everything in Mrs. Gilly's house was as warm and welcoming as Mrs. Gilly herself. It seemed that Poppy had everything she could ever want. The dog scampered into the room and snuffled through a basket of toys beside the couch, her tail wagging. She emerged with a floppy stuffed monkey and dropped it in Mrs. Gilly's lap.

"She *tries* to be a good dog, but sometimes I wonder if I'm helping in the best way I can." Mrs. Gilly scratched Poppy under the chin. The dog closed her eyes and leaned against Mrs. Gilly's leg.

"What do you mean?" Hannah asked.

"I rescued Poppy because I wanted to give her a better home." Mrs. Gilly tossed the stuffed monkey toward the dining room, and Poppy scrambled after it, then brought it right back. "You should've seen her in the shelter," Mrs. Gilly said. "The other dogs were either anxious and barking or so scared that they huddled in the back of their kennels and tried to disappear. But not Poppy. She wasn't the slightest bit jumpy, even though she was a stray who'd been on the streets. She sat right at the front of her crate, just as proper and polite as possible, hoping someone would stop to pet her. She was so sweet and calm." Mrs. Gilly gave Poppy a loving look. "Weren't you, dear?"

Poppy froze, the monkey lodged in her strong jaw, and cast her eyes up at Mrs. Gilly. They stared at each other for a second; then Poppy hopped up and spun in a circle, flinging her head—and the monkey—from side to side. Mrs. Gilly and Hannah laughed. It was hard for Hannah to imagine Poppy being calm. As far as she could tell, the pup never stopped wriggling.

"I knew instantly that Poppy has a huge heart," Mrs.

Gilly went on. "When she smiled at me, it was as bright as the California sunshine, and I couldn't believe that everyone else ignored her or looked scared and just walked on by."

"Why? Because people are scared of pit bulls?" Hannah asked.

Mrs. Gilly nodded. "Exactly, so they don't want to adopt them."

Hannah thought back to Sophia's reaction to Poppy. It was sad to see that such a kind dog was so misunderstood.

"But Poppy's just a puppy," Hannah said. "She's not dangerous—she's just . . . high-energy."

"She is most certainly that." Mrs. Gilly's expression turned sad. "And when I adopted her, I never expected that I was going to need hip surgery. Puppies need endless exercise, plus constant guidance and structure to learn how to behave. But I can't even take her for walks." She paused for a long moment. The two of them sat in silence, watching Poppy hold the monkey between her two front paws while she licked its head. When Mrs. Gilly spoke again, her voice wavered. "It breaks my heart, but if I can't get Poppy well trained, I won't be able to keep her. That just wouldn't be fair to her."

Her words sank into Hannah like heavy weights.

"But if she goes back to the shelter," Mrs. Gilly finished, "I worry that people will walk right by her kennel again—and then who knows what could happen to her."

Hannah's breath caught in her throat. "But you can't give her up! This is her home."

"That's the last thing I want to do," Mrs. Gilly said. "I love Poppy very much. But if I can't train her, then I can't help her overcome her bad reputation."

That gave Hannah an idea. *She* could be the person who helped train Poppy, played with her, and took her for walks. Then, by the time school started, Mrs. Gilly would be able to take care of her again. Hannah's parents wanted her to spend more time out of the house this summer, didn't they? What could be better than helping a neighbor and getting to spend more time with Poppy? Poppy was so lucky she'd been rescued by Mrs. Gilly, and now they loved each other —they *had* to stay together! Plus Poppy was the only thing Hannah liked in California. She couldn't imagine losing her now.

"What if I helped train Poppy?" Hannah scooted to the edge of the couch, the whole plan unfolding in her mind. "Then could you keep her?"

Mrs. Gilly raised her eyebrows. "Have you ever trained a dog?"

Hannah didn't know the first thing about dog training. But Poppy seemed smart, and she had come running when Hannah called her name. How hard could it be? Hannah had lots of time to figure it out before sixth grade started.

"No, but I can learn. And—" Hannah didn't get to finish saying how much she loved animals. Or how she and Linnea had helped Linnea's grandparents at their farm one summer, even learning how to get the chickens back into their coop at night. She was interrupted by Poppy barking excitedly.

Poppy ran to the front window, her tail whipping back and forth. Her loud, deep barks filled the room as she smeared nose prints on the glass. Hannah got up to see what Poppy was all worked up about and saw Sophia and her family walking down the street. Hannah cringed—she'd totally forgotten that they were at her house. Her mom was not going to be happy that she hadn't come right home.

Sophia must have heard the barking through the window. She glanced up from her phone long enough to shoot a look over her shoulder at Poppy. Hannah almost ducked out of sight, but then realized that she could use this moment to start training Poppy and help Mrs. Gilly.

"Poppy, come here. That's enough barking," Hannah said. She hoped the dog would respond instantly, as she had in the yard, but this time Poppy ignored her. She put her paws up on the windowsill and kept sounding the alarm. Hannah's heart started to pound a little faster—how could she stop Poppy from barking? She thought quickly. When one of the twins was crying, she could usually get him to quiet down by distracting him with one of their toys. Maybe the same thing would work with the dog.

Hannah crossed the room and grabbed the stuffed monkey from the floor. She squeezed it until she found the squeaker. That got Poppy's attention. Poppy turned from the window and cocked her head at the sound, one ear pricked up and the other dangling downward. Hannah waggled the toy, luring Poppy away from the window. Then she tossed it toward the dining room, and Poppy bounded after it, forgetting all about the scene outside. Poppy brought it back, and Hannah scratched her behind the ears.

"Good girl," Hannah said.

They played this game until Sophia and her family turned the corner toward their house and were out of sight. Then Hannah tossed the toy one more time and sat down on the couch again. Poppy picked up the monkey and, carrying it in her mouth, ran over to check the window. She scanned the street, but this time she stayed quiet.

"That was some quick thinking," Mrs. Gilly said with a smile, watching from the couch. "Taking control of situations like that is an important part of training a dog. I can tell you have a lot of confidence in you. I think this might work, Hannah—or at least I'm willing to try."

Hannah suddenly felt self-conscious. She looked down at her knees and let her hair fall over her face. She wasn't used to taking compliments, and she wasn't sure she had as much confidence as Mrs. Gilly seemed to think—but she was sure she didn't want Poppy to go back to the shelter.

She found her voice. "I'd really like to try."

Mrs. Gilly nodded. "You'd have to work with Poppy every day to teach her and practice with her."

"That sounds like fun." And Hannah meant it. "Come here, Poppy!"

The dog trotted over and dropped the monkey at Hannah's feet. Hannah picked it up and tossed it. Poppy leaped up, caught it in her teeth, and started shaking it, her ears flapping wildly.

"But there's something very important you need to remember, Hannah," Mrs. Gilly said, her voice serious. "Poppy can't just be a good dog. She needs to be the *best* dog."

Hannah thought of Sophia bragging about her *perfect* puppy, Louie the Goldendoodle. Why should he get all the training and attention? If Louie was going to training class, then Poppy was going to go too. Poppy deserved to have people love her as much as they loved Louie.

Poppy pranced over to the recliner with her prize. She flopped down next to Mrs. Gilly's walker to chew on it.

Hannah lifted her chin and met Mrs. Gilly's gaze. "I think she's already the best. And we'll prove it."

★ CHAPTER 5 ★

When Hannah got home from Mrs. Gilly's house, the dishes from brunch were piled in the sink. Her mom was outside, practicing soccer with Jenny, and her dad was putting the twins down for a nap. It wasn't officially Hannah's job to do the dishes, but if she didn't, they might still be sitting there by bedtime.

As Hannah rinsed bits of egg and fruit off the plates, she imagined herself getting Poppy to do all kinds of tricks. Linnea's cousin had a dog who knew how to shake and roll over, and he put all his toys back in the basket when he was told to "clean up." Hannah could teach Poppy to give high-fives with her paw or to fetch things for Mrs. Gilly. She had no idea how she'd teach Poppy all these things, but she'd figure it out. If Poppy were perfectly trained, people would give her a chance, and Mrs. Gilly could keep her, and that's all that mattered.

When the dishes were lined up in the dishwasher, Hannah looked up dog tricks on the Internet. She spent the afternoon watching videos of dogs running through obstacle courses and jumping through hoops. She imagined that Poppy would have fun doing these things. She just needed to get her parents' permission to start dog training, and she had the perfect way to get them to agree.

★ ★ ★

As Hannah scooped Kung Pao tofu onto the pile of rice on her plate, she kept thinking of all the ways she could train Poppy.

"Hannah! Pass the lo mein to your father." Her mom's voice had that *this isn't the first time I've asked you for the noodles* tone. Jenny's eyes went wide, like she was about to witness her sister getting into trouble.

Hannah snapped out of her dog-training fantasy. "Sorry." She quickly passed the cardboard carton to her dad.

"You've had your head in the clouds all day," her dad said, taking a big scoop of noodles for himself and dropping a smaller scoop on Jenny's plate. "Is everything okay?"

Hannah knew this was her chance. She took a deep breath and set down her chopsticks. "You know how you've been wanting me to get out of the house more this summer?"

Her parents nodded. Logan started throwing Cheerios at Noah. Hannah knew she had to talk fast before the twins distracted her parents. "Well, I found something I really, really want to do. Mrs. Gilly has to use her walker for the whole summer, and she needs my help."

"Help doing what?" her mom asked.

"Training Poppy." Hannah's voice rose with excitement, and her words spilled out all at once. "She's a really good dog, but she needs to be trained, and it's hard for Mrs. Gilly to work with her since she can't walk her. But Poppy likes me, and I know I can teach her." She took a breath and glanced from her mom to her dad and back again.

Her parents exchanged a look, and Hannah's heart began to sink even before they spoke. She knew she had to put her last card on the table quickly. "I was thinking I could even take Poppy to training classes with Sophia and her puppy . . . if you want me to." It was the last thing Hannah wanted to promise, but she knew it was the only way her parents would agree to her helping Mrs. Gilly.

"That's very sweet and generous of you," her mom said.

"Sophia is so cool," Jenny piped in. "After you left, she showed us videos of her and her friends surfing."

Hannah made a face at her sister when her parents weren't looking. Jenny was *supposed* to be on her side.

"It's just that—wouldn't you rather be spending time at the beach with Sophia than at a doggy training camp?"

"I could do that, too—but, Mom, if Mrs. Gilly can't

train her," Hannah said, feeling her face starting to turn red, "she might not be able to keep her, and she really loves Poppy."

As she spoke, Hannah realized that she was also falling in love with the big, sweet puppy. She'd been surprised at the immediate connection between them, yet it was almost as if she and Poppy had known each other for a long time. She couldn't have a dog of her own—her parents were already overwhelmed enough with the twins—but with Poppy next door, it was basically like Hannah having a dog, too. If she was going to be stuck in California, that might just make things a little more tolerable.

Her dad's expression softened. "Mrs. Gilly does seem to love that dog. That would break her heart. But"—he turned back to Hannah—"this is your summer vacation! Are you sure you want to spend it with a badly trained dog and an elderly neighbor?"

Hannah saw a glimmer of hope. This was her chance. "Poppy isn't a bad dog, Dad. She just needs help. Please—I *want* to do this—" She tried not to sound like she was begging. "I really want to spend the summer with Poppy."

The twins started squealing, and the conversation was put on hold while Hannah's parents freed them from their highchairs. Her mom's brow was furrowed, as if she were pondering something serious. Hannah nudged the rest of her rice and sauce into the shape of a little mountain, too excited and nervous to eat any more.

Her mom bounced Noah on her lap and looked across the table at Hannah. She opened her mouth to speak, and Hannah held her breath. "I'll call Mrs. Lin after dinner and see if you can still join the obedience class," her mom said.

"Thank you, Mom!" Spending time with Sophia wasn't exactly what Hannah wanted, but it was better than not being able to train Poppy at all.

"What if Poppy goes crazy?" Jenny asked. "She's a scary dog."

"No, she's not," Hannah said. "You're only saying that because you heard Sophia say it. I'll bring Poppy over so you can meet her. You'll see how sweet she is."

"Okay!" Jenny grinned. "Maybe I can play soccer with her."

"Sure." Hannah pictured Poppy running circles around Jenny with the ball in her mouth.

"Hang on a second." Hannah's dad raised his hand like a referee calling a foul. "There's something else we need to discuss."

All eyes turned to him.

"Poppy is a pit bull mix, and we don't know much about her," he went on. "We need to be careful around the twins."

Hannah's mouth dropped open. "But you've seen how nice she is, Dad."

"I saw a big, rowdy dog run through our yard today." He leaned his elbows on the table and looked at Hannah intently. "We don't want to stand in your way, Hannah. But you need to be conscious of the dog's reputation. We just don't want anyone to get hurt."

Her mom sighed and nodded. "Your dad has a good point, Hannah. You'll need to be really careful."

Hannah couldn't believe that her dad was judging Poppy for being a pit bull—and that her mom was going along with it. He'd seen how friendly she was, and he'd even said he knew how much Mrs. Gilly loved the dog. Would Mrs. Gilly feel that way about a dangerous animal? No way.

Mrs. Gilly was right about people not giving Poppy a chance. But Hannah was worried that if she argued, her parents might change their minds about the dog training. So she bit her tongue and slumped in her chair, letting her hair fall across her face. She'd get to see Poppy again tomorrow, and everything would be better.

★ CHAPTER 6 ★

Obedience class took place in a big field at a local park. A ramp and some hurdles were set up from an earlier advanced training class. Hannah had seen videos online of dogs leaping over them. But as Poppy tugged on her leash and jumped excitedly against Hannah's legs, Hannah realized that they had a long way to go before Poppy would be ready for obstacle courses and tricks.

Sophia was crouched down by Louie, scratching his fluffy reddish-blond ears. She stood quickly as Hannah and Poppy got closer.

"Hi," Sophia said. She wrapped Louie's leash tighter around her hand and eyed Poppy warily.

Hannah closed her eyes, took a slow breath, and tried to ignore Sophia's obvious discomfort. She had decided on the way over that she and Poppy were going to make a good first impression in class, so she needed to focus. Pushing away the memory of the mean things Sophia had said about Poppy, Hannah pretended that Sophia's greeting had been friendlier than it really was.

"Hi, Sophia." Hannah forced herself to smile. "This must be Louie. He's so adorable!"

"Thanks." Sophia seemed to relax the tiniest bit, but she still wouldn't look at Hannah. "He's really smart, too. He already knows lots of commands."

Hannah wanted to brag about what Poppy knew, but the dog was straining against her leash to get closer to Louie. When she couldn't reach the other dog, Poppy spun around and, in the next second, almost tackled Hannah by jumping up on her.

"Poppy, *off!*" Hannah took a step backwards to catch her balance and gently pushed the dog off her. It took three tries before Poppy got all four feet on the ground. Hannah tried to brush the dirty paw prints off her T-shirt, but she only smeared the dirt around. So much for her first impression.

When Hannah looked up, Sophia and Louie had moved away from them. Aside from Poppy and Louie, there were three other dogs in class. A shiny black lab mix weaved back and forth between two young men, nosing their hands for attention. A small, scruffy terrier mix huddled nervously against the legs of a woman who stood stiffly in dress pants and a button-down shirt, looking like it was her first time in a park. She eyed each of the dogs suspiciously, but Hannah noticed that her gaze lingered on Poppy for a second longer than the others. A big black and brown German shepherd sat beside a teenage girl with short black hair and a dozen ear piercings, both of them watching everyone else with cool, unreadable expressions.

The shorter of the two men, who had broad shoulders and spiky hair, came over to say hi to Poppy. He let her jump up and lick his chin. "Wow, and I thought Cleo had a lot of energy," he said, laughing.

That was the understatement of the year. Poppy seemed to have way more energy than all the other dogs combined.

"She's still a puppy," Hannah said, trying not to sound as defensive as she felt. She knew it was a silly thing to say, since all the dogs seemed to be about the same age.

"She looks like a handful, but she's cute. My sister has one, too." He patted Poppy once more and headed back to his partner and their dog. Hannah wasn't sure if he meant his sister had a pit bull or a handful, but at least he'd noticed how cute Poppy was.

Poppy tugged hard on her leash as he walked away, desperate to follow him. All the new people and sights and sounds had her really worked up. Her ears twitched and her whole body shook with excitement.

Holding tightly to the leash, Hannah picked up a stick

from the ground and tried to distract her with it, but the pup wasn't interested. Poppy just wanted to have fun, which meant that Hannah wanted to disappear into the background. She'd expected the beginning obedience class to be filled with other dogs who needed as much training as Poppy did. But class hadn't even started yet and Poppy was clearly the least well-behaved dog there.

Maybe they should just leave and do this whole training thing on their own, when no one was watching. Maybe Mrs. Gilly could help her one-on-one.

Hannah dropped the stick, feeling defeated. After a moment she felt someone watching her, and when she looked up, she caught Sophia's eye from across the grass. Sophia looked away quickly, but Louie stood up on his back legs and pulled against his leash, trying to get to Poppy. Poppy barked happily at Louie and splayed her front legs, then dropped her chest to the ground.

Sophia wasn't having it. She gave her dog one tiny tug, and he sat right back down on his rump, watching Poppy quietly from afar. Meanwhile, Poppy's desire to play had only gotten stronger. She barked and yipped at Louie and pulled so hard on her leash that Hannah was sure her shoulder was going to be sore the next day.

But there was no way Hannah was going to let Sophia see her give up so easily.

"Poppy, look what I've got for you!" Hannah reached into the pouch clipped around her waist, which Mrs. Gilly had filled with tiny bits of chopped-up hot dog. She tried to use the happy voice Mrs. Gilly had shown her to get Poppy's attention, but her voice came out as a squeak. Poppy smelled the food anyway and bounded back to Hannah as if her leash were a rubber band. She gobbled up the treat and looked at Hannah for more. Poppy was panting, her tail wagged, and her whole body hummed with excitement.

"Good girl." Hannah patted the spot on Poppy's head that she thought of as her birthmark. Then she leaned down and whispered in the dog's ear. "We can do this, Poppy. We *have* to do this."

Poppy licked Hannah's cheek. Hannah decided to take that as a sign of agreement.

A sharp whistle drew everyone's attention to the center of the circle. A short woman with red hair stood with her hands on her hips, waiting for the people and the dogs to quiet down. Her wide, friendly smile put Hannah at ease. Hannah could imagine the trainer's calm confidence rubbing off on her — and on Poppy.

"My name is Marcy, and I'm here to train *you* to train your dog. But first I'd like to get to know you guys a bit. Let's go around the circle. Introduce yourselves — that includes canines — and tell us one thing you love about your dog and one thing you hope they'll learn in class. Why don't you start?" She pointed at the woman with the terrier.

"I'm Carol, and this is Trixie." Carol's mouth was pursed, as if she had just eaten something sour. She scanned the group, sizing up the others as if she were cataloging all the ways her dog was better than theirs. "I love when Trixie curls up by my feet when we watch TV in the evenings, but it drives me crazy that she pulls me down the street every time we go for a walk."

Hannah had a hard time picturing the small dog pulling anyone anywhere.

Marcy nodded. "Great. We'll definitely work on loose-leash walking. Next?"

"I'm Josh." The taller of the young men pushed his wire-rimmed glasses up on his nose, then nodded at the man with the spiky hair. "This is David. And we just adopted Cleo two weeks ago. She's amazing. She loves everyone but definitely needs to work on her manners." Cleo let out a short bark, as if she knew they were talking about her.

"You're in the right place," Marcy said.

The teenage girl went next. She didn't seem nervous at all about going after the adults. Meanwhile, Hannah could barely listen to what everyone else was saying as she thought about her turn. She didn't know what to say. Poppy wasn't even her dog, not really. She didn't want to tell everyone Mrs.

Gilly's life story. And with Poppy's attention flitting from Hannah to the other dogs to people playing on the other side of the park, it was obvious that they needed a lot of help.

"My name's Jess, and this is Sierra," the girl said as her dog looked up at her, watching her silently. "She kind of seems to know what I want her to do even before I ask, but I want to teach her real commands and cool tricks. Maybe eventually do agility with her."

Jess and Sierra seemed to have such a close bond. Hannah could picture the two of them on one of those agility obstacle courses she'd seen online.

Sophia was up next. She fidgeted with Louie's leash as she talked. "I'm Sophia, and this is Louie. I love how playful Louie is, but sometimes he steals my stuff instead of playing with his toys."

Hannah was surprised. Perfect Louie was a trouble-maker after all!

"We'll work on that, too," Marcy promised. "Last, but not least. It's Poppy, right?"

Poppy jerked on the leash when she heard her name, and Hannah had to brace herself so she didn't get pulled over. Everyone in class was staring at them, their hands wrapped tightly around their dogs' leashes, making sure their own dogs stayed close by their sides. Did they think Poppy was going to attack?

Embarrassment flooding through her, Hannah ducked her head so her hair fell over her birthmark. But then Poppy tugged her in another direction and Hannah's hair flew around as she tried to get Poppy back under control. Now she was sure people were staring at her face *and* at her hyper dog. A trickle of sweat dripped down the side of her forehead, but she didn't want anyone to see her wiping it away. For the second time in just a few minutes, she began to wonder if this had been a mistake. Maybe she could just walk away and call her mom to pick her and Poppy up.

Marcy stepped closer and distracted Poppy with a treat. She gave Hannah an encouraging smile. "She's such a cute dog. Why don't you tell us a little about her?"

"I'm . . . I'm Hannah," she managed to say. "And this is Poppy. She was adopted from the shelter. She's really sweet, but kind of wild sometimes." Hannah's words came out soft and rushed. She wasn't even sure how many people could hear her, but she immediately felt guilty for saying anything bad about Poppy. She wished she'd said something different, so the other dog owners wouldn't get the wrong idea. But it was too late.

"Training will help with her energy," Marcy said. "It makes dogs more focused and wears them out because they have to think about what they're doing." She moved back to the middle of the group. "We're going to start easy—by reintroducing yourself to your dog. Call their name, then give them a treat when they look at you. We want them to associate good things with their name."

Hannah was relieved that they were starting with something so simple. Poppy already knew this. Whenever Hannah or Mrs. Gilly said her name, even if it was just in conversation, Poppy lifted her head and tilted it to one side as if she were listening. Now that hot dogs were involved, it was even easier to get her attention. Hannah relaxed and said Poppy's name. Sure enough, Poppy did her adorable head tilt and Hannah gave her a treat. After she'd swallowed it whole, Poppy watched Hannah as if she were the only person in the world, waiting to see what she'd do next. For the first time all morning, Hannah remembered why she'd wanted to do this in the first place.

Marcy was making the rounds as they practiced. Poppy saw her coming, and suddenly this new person was way more interesting than another bite of hot dog. She leaped toward Marcy, yanking the leash out of Hannah's hand. Before Hannah could even call Poppy's name, Marcy caught the nylon strap by the loop end. Poppy was so strong, Hannah was worried she'd knock Marcy down, but the trainer lowered the leash to the ground and stepped on it, forcing

Poppy to stop jumping. Once the dog was a bit calmer, Marcy picked up the leash and handed it back to Hannah. "Make sure you hang on to her."

Hannah was mortified. She was sure her cheeks must be bright red, her birthmark an alarming shade of purple. With the hand that wasn't clenching Poppy's leash with white knuckles, she swept her hair back in front of her face. She couldn't bring herself to meet Marcy's eyes as she mumbled thank you.

"It's okay," Marcy said. "It happens to everyone."

But it hadn't happened to everyone. It had only happened to Hannah. She could hear the other people in class calling their dogs' names over and over. It had been for only a second, but she was sure they'd all seen Poppy pull away from her.

Marcy took a treat out of her own pouch and with a few quick hand movements she had Poppy sitting and completely focused. Marcy gave Poppy the treat and scratched behind her ears. "She's a smart girl. You'll have her trained in no time, but you have to try not to get upset—she can sense it."

"Okay, I'll try," Hannah said. But she didn't see how it was possible not to be upset. She was doing the worst job ever at training Poppy. She'd sworn to Mrs. Gilly and her parents that she could do this, but halfway through her first class she was already failing. Everyone else in class just wanted a better-behaved dog, but Hannah needed to get Poppy under control so she could stay with Mrs. Gilly— and not get sent back to the shelter.

It was the most important thing Hannah had ever done.

"Just have confidence." Marcy smiled and patted Hannah on the shoulder, a bit like she'd patted Poppy.

There was that word again, Hannah thought. *Confidence*. Marcy wanted her to have it, and Mrs. Gilly had said she'd seen it in her, but Hannah wasn't feeling it. She looked down at Poppy, who gazed up at Hannah lovingly, her tail swiping back and forth across the grass. She grinned as if she were having a blast.

Hannah sighed at the dog. Her hand was getting sore from gripping Poppy's leash so tightly, but she wasn't going to risk dropping it again.

Marcy called for their attention. "Now we're going to teach your dogs how to sit on command. Hannah, could you bring Poppy over here to help me demonstrate?"

Hannah's palms started sweating as she walked into the center of the circle. Poppy bounded alongside her, tail wagging. The dog was thrilled to be in the middle of the action, but Hannah wished she could hide behind a tree. So much for confidence—she felt so self-conscious about her birthmark and about Poppy jumping up on the trainer that she couldn't even pay attention to the instructions. She hadn't expected that dog training was going to put her smack-dab in the center of everything. She'd wanted the opposite, just her and Poppy.

Using a firm but not harsh voice, Marcy got Poppy to sit a few times, then nodded at Hannah. "Okay, your turn."

It took Hannah a few tries just to get a piece of hot dog out of the pouch. Her fingers were greasy from the treats and Poppy's slobber. Frustration rose in her chest, and blood started to pound in her ears. She dropped a treat into the grass and Poppy scarfed up the freebie. Once she managed to get a chunk of meat between her fingers, Hannah held it above Poppy's nose the way Marcy had. "Poppy, sit!"

Poppy sat up on her hind legs and tried to nibble the treat out of Hannah's hand. She dropped to the ground and backed up instead of sitting. She wiggled and hopped. She looked at Hannah and barked. The worst part was that Poppy *knew* this command—she'd just done it for Marcy, and she sat perfectly for Mrs. Gilly at home all the time! But with everyone's eyes on them, Poppy acted as if she'd never even heard the word. Hannah was so frustrated, she was almost yelling the word *sit*, even though she knew she should be copying Marcy's calm tone. It didn't make any difference.

Marcy took pity on Hannah and let her and Poppy go

back to their spot. Hannah was so embarrassed, she felt like crying. The trainer called Louie and Sophia to the center and demonstrated the hand movement again. Of course Louie sat right away.

Marcy told everyone to practice with their dogs, but Hannah's throat felt tight. Distracted by everyone else, she could barely get the word *sit* out. Carol's shrill voice cut through Hannah's concentration as she singsonged the command at Trixie. Josh and David were laughing like they were playing a game with Cleo. Jess and Sierra went through the exercise as if they'd done it a million times before. Hannah's back was to Sophia, but she could hear her telling Louie over and over again what a good boy he was.

As Hannah kept trying to get Poppy to sit, Poppy seemed to be getting more and more confused. She finally sat on her own and looked up at Hannah, her brow furrowed and her head cocked to the side, as if asking what was wrong.

"Everything is wrong," Hannah muttered. "How am I ever going to train you?"

"You're doing great," Marcy said. Hannah hadn't noticed her coming back around the circle. "Shelter dogs often need a little extra patience. Poppy has probably had to go through a lot of changes. But she clearly trusts you, so you have a good foundation."

Marcy was like Mrs. Gilly—she seemed to accept both

Poppy and Hannah for who they were. But Hannah wasn't so sure about everyone else in class. She swore she could feel them sneaking glances at her birthmark and judging Poppy for being a pit bull. As Marcy walked away to help Josh and David, Hannah felt tears spring to her eyes. She squeezed her eyelids shut to keep them from spilling over.

Poppy nudged Hannah's hand with her wet nose. "I don't have any more hot dog," Hannah said. Poppy yipped at her, and Hannah opened her eyes. To her surprise, Poppy didn't seem to be looking for a snack after all—she didn't have that slightly frantic *where's my treat?* look on her face. Instead, she was watching Hannah with big, round eyes and whining softly. Hannah squatted down and put an arm around her, and Poppy nuzzled against her and sniffed her face, as if checking for tears in Hannah's eyes.

Hannah let out an astonished laugh. The dog, she realized, was worried about her.

"Poppy," she said. "You sweet thing."

It was almost as if Poppy could sense that right then, Hannah needed her as much as she needed Hannah.

The other dog owners were probably staring again, but Hannah didn't care. She felt as though it were just her and Poppy in the park. Hannah might be shy, while Poppy was outgoing—but they were in this together. Hannah reminded herself that this was only their first day. She and

Poppy were both in a new place, surrounded by new people. It was going to take some time for them to adjust.

Besides, Hannah thought, she was used to the stares by now. It always took a while for her to get used to strangers, and for them to get used to her. Maybe it would be the same for Poppy. Maybe, because she was a pit bull and had so much energy, people didn't immediately love her, but that didn't stop Poppy from loving everyone she met.

"You're a good dog." Hannah leaned over and kissed Poppy's nose. "We outsiders have to stick together. I'm going to make sure you don't go back to the shelter."

★ CHAPTER 7 ★

Hannah waited for everyone else in class to leave the park. She'd had enough of being in the spotlight and didn't want them all watching Poppy yank her down the sidewalk.

Mrs. Lin arrived to pick up Sophia and Louie. "Do you and Poppy need a ride home?" she asked.

"No, thank you," Hannah said. "My mom was all right with me walking home. It's not that far, and Poppy could still use the exercise."

"Okay, well, we'll see you tomorrow, then!" Mrs. Lin said.

"What's tomorrow?" Hannah asked.

"Didn't your mom tell you?"

Hannah shook her head.

"We invited you to the beach with Sophia and her friends." Mrs. Lin wrinkled her forehead. "Your mom said you'd love to go. I hope that's okay?"

Hannah couldn't believe their moms had decided to set up another "playdate" for them. Between the disastrous brunch and obedience school, wasn't that enough? She glanced at Sophia, who was looking down at Louie. At least she wasn't glaring or shaking her head, so maybe she'd agreed to introduce Hannah to her friends. Hannah couldn't back out now.

"Of course," she said to Mrs. Lin, knowing she didn't have much of a choice. "I can't wait!"

"Great. Well, enjoy your walk home. It's a beautiful day."

Hannah didn't understand why adults always commented on the weather. As far as she could tell, the weather was beautiful every day in California. It would be beautiful again tomorrow for her beach day, even if Hannah felt like a gloomy cloud being stuck with Sophia again.

Hannah forced a smile. "Thanks, Mrs. Lin. Bye, Sophia."

"Bye." Sophia lifted the hand holding Louie's leash in a little wave. Her mom shot her a look, and she added, "See you tomorrow."

Hannah watched Sophia and her mom walk to their car, Louie trotting between them. Sophia's phone was out before they even made it out of the parking spot. She was probably sending another update to all her friends about the awkward new girl and her out-of-control dog. Hannah sighed. Now she had to meet all those friends in real life tomorrow. But at least, for the next few blocks, she had some one-on-one time with Poppy. That was worth a beach day with Sophia.

As they walked home, Hannah tried to relax and enjoy the moment. But Poppy kept tugging excitedly, and Hannah was worried that the dog might drag her all the way home. Then Hannah decided that maybe if she picked up her pace, Poppy could run alongside. Hannah took off at a trot, her sneakers sweeping over the pavement, and a happy Poppy bounded next to her, matching her speed. Hannah's hair flew behind her as she and Poppy ran down the sidewalk, passing people gardening and kids playing in yards. Dogs barked at them from behind fences, but Poppy ignored them. She was too distracted and they were going too fast for her to bark in response.

When they reached the top of a hill halfway between the park and their street, Hannah paused to catch her breath. The ocean glittered on the horizon, and a salty breeze blew across her face. She and Poppy panted in rhythm with each other. Poppy dropped to the ground and rolled on her back on the sidewalk, then flopped onto her stomach, her mouth open in a big grin. It was impossible for Hannah not to smile. She felt her shoulders relax. No one was watching or judging them there. It felt like heaven.

"You're a good girl," Hannah said to Poppy. "I know you're trying, and I won't give up on you."

Poppy's tail brushed back and forth on the pavement.

"Ready to head home?" Hannah asked. "I'll race you."

Poppy leaped to her feet.

They took off down the hill, Poppy galloping beside Hannah, her tongue flopping out of her mouth with joy. Hannah felt a smile of her own break out across her face. They ran until they reached the end of their street; then Hannah slowed to a walk so they could both cool down. Poppy trotted by her side, her extra energy burned off by the run. Hannah could feel her own heart pounding, from both the race and her love for Poppy.

Mrs. Gilly was waiting on her front porch, sipping a glass of iced tea. Hannah started to feel nervous again. She just knew Mrs. Gilly was going to ask *How was class?* the way her parents did every day after school. How was she supposed to explain what a terrible student Poppy had been? What if Mrs. Gilly decided that Hannah wasn't cut out for dog training?

But instead Mrs. Gilly said, "Come inside. Show me what you two learned today."

Mrs. Gilly moved slowly as she maneuvered her walker across the porch, through the front door, and into the living room. Poppy patiently walked by her owner's side and stood guard while Mrs. Gilly settled into her recliner with a sharp exhale. Hannah took it as a great sign that Poppy hadn't jumped up on Mrs. Gilly or tried to knock her over—the dog was too tired! Maybe that could be the trick to training her. If she got out all her energy, she'd be less rambunctious and ready to listen to all her commands.

With a million new ideas going through her head, Hannah followed them inside and stood in the middle of the room. Both Poppy and Mrs. Gilly watched her expectantly. She swallowed and wiped her hands on her shorts.

"Do you have any treats?" Hannah asked. "We used up all the hot dog, and I'm not sure Poppy can do the commands without them yet."

"Of course!" Mrs. Gilly said. "She's still learning. There's a jar in the kitchen."

Hannah hurried down the hall and found the jar with the bone-shaped knob on the lid. The treats inside were small and crunchy. They looked like boring dog kibble. Hannah wasn't sure they'd be exciting enough after the bits of hot dog she'd used in class, but she shoved a handful in the treat pouch and returned to the living room.

"Okay, Poppy! You ready?" Hannah pushed away her nervousness and tried to channel Marcy's calm confidence. She thought about the sun on her face at the top of the hill, and how happy and free she had felt during their run home.

Poppy looked up at her. Hannah took out a treat and said, "Poppy, sit."

Poppy sat before Hannah finished giving her the hand signal.

"Good girl!" Hannah gave Poppy the treat. She moved around the living room and asked Poppy to sit on her dog bed, by the fireplace, and next to the couch. Poppy sat every time. She even waited almost thirty seconds in a sitting position until Hannah said "okay" to release her.

"That's wonderful!" Mrs. Gilly clapped with delight after Hannah released Poppy from an extra-long sit by the window.

"The trainer told us to practice in lots of different places and for different amounts of time to help our dogs remember the commands," Hannah said. She wasn't nervous anymore, or embarrassed to be working with Poppy in front of Mrs. Gilly. Maybe it was because Mrs. Gilly wasn't a stranger, though it didn't hurt that Poppy was acting like the perfect dog.

"I wonder if she'd do it without a treat," Mrs. Gilly said. "Why don't you give it a try?"

"Um, okay." Hannah took a deep breath and called Poppy over to her in the middle of the room. With nothing in her hand, she gave the signal and said, "Poppy, sit!"

Poppy looked at her for a second, as if pondering the

suggestion; then she sat. Hannah bent down and scratched the dog behind her collar. "You did it! You're a genius."

Poppy licked the tip of Hannah's nose, making her and Mrs. Gilly laugh.

"What else did you learn?" Mrs. Gilly asked.

Hannah wiped the dog slobber off her nose with the back of her hand. She took out another treat and lured Poppy into a down position. She showed off the command a few more times, then stood and faced Mrs. Gilly. She tucked her hair behind her ears as she explained, "We just did *sit* and *down* today. We also talked a lot about how to communicate with our dogs and how training works. I think next time we'll work on *stay* and walking on a leash."

Mrs. Gilly nodded. "Excellent work, you two."

As Hannah and Mrs. Gilly talked, Poppy curled up on her dog bed, her nose tucked under her paw, and dozed off. It was hard to believe this was the same dog who had been leaping all over Hannah in class.

Hannah dropped to the rug next to Poppy's bed. Poppy sighed and shifted to rest her head on Hannah's knee.

"You and Poppy must be at the top of the class," Mrs. Gilly said proudly.

Not quite, Hannah thought. But she didn't want to admit that to Mrs. Gilly, not after Poppy had just shown how well she could listen. Hannah looked down at the sleepy dog and rubbed the soft fur on Poppy's snout with her fingertips. Poppy was exhausted—and totally calm. She just needed to get her puppy energy out so she could focus.

How could Hannah get Poppy to act like this all the time?

"We're working on it," Hannah said. Poppy yawned and let out a little squeak, and Hannah realized that she felt just as tired as the dog. As training class and the run home caught up with her, she was tempted to lie down next to Poppy on the soft dog bed. She was discovering just how much work puppies could be.

★ CHAPTER 8 ★

Hannah sat on the front porch, her hat jammed low on her head, wondering what she was about to get herself into. A canvas beach bag stuffed with a striped orange towel, even more sunscreen, and a water bottle sat by her feet.

A Prius pulled into the driveway with Mrs. Lin behind the wheel and Sophia in the passenger seat, tapping away on her phone. Strapped to the car's roof was a long white surfboard that gleamed in the sunshine. Hannah had to admit that it was nice of Mrs. Lin to drive them—it'd have been easy to walk to the beach, but less so with Sophia's giant surfboard. With a big sigh, Hannah picked up her beach bag and trudged down the porch steps to the car.

Mrs. Lin started chatting before Hannah had even buckled her seat belt. "It looked like you had your hands full at obedience class. That was Mrs. Gilly's dog, right?"

"Yes. I'm training Poppy. She's a really good dog," Hannah said.

"I'm so glad you and Sophia are in class together. Maybe Louie and Poppy will become friends, too."

Hannah thought Sophia might have rolled her eyes, but it was hard to tell from the back seat. Mrs. Lin changed topics. "Are you excited to spend the afternoon at the beach?"

"Sure," Hannah answered cheerfully. She couldn't help acting polite and enthusiastic around adults. It wasn't that she didn't like the beach. She loved going to the lake with Linnea and their other friends in the summer and swimming in the cool water. But the only person she'd know at this beach was Sophia—who honestly didn't seem that excited to have Hannah tagging along. And as beautiful as the ocean was, Hannah was afraid to go into the water with its huge, crashing waves.

"You'll finally get to meet Sophia's friends," Mrs. Lin said, as if she'd read Hannah's mind. Hannah had a hard time feeling excited about meeting the other girls. She could only guess what Sophia had told them about her, and if Sophia's friends were as rude as she was, it was going to be a miserable afternoon. Mrs. Lin kept on chatting about how much everyone loved the beach, how amazing the waves were, and her favorite ice cream place on the boardwalk.

She didn't seem to notice that Hannah didn't respond, or that Sophia hadn't said a single word since Hannah had gotten into the car.

A few minutes later they pulled into the sandy parking lot. Sophia untied the surfboard from the roof of the car. When it was free, she stepped away from the car and said, "Bye, Mom!"

Hannah was surprised to see that Sophia was beaming as her mom drove away. Sophia always looked like she belonged, but with her tan skin and black ponytail, and the board tucked beneath her arm, she really seemed at home on the beach. Sophia started toward the water, then turned back. "Are you coming?" she asked impatiently.

Hannah hitched her beach bag onto her shoulder and followed. They'd made it only a few feet through the deep sand when two girls started waving wildly at them. The girls had already laid out their oversize towels, which were strewn with magazines and snacks. Surfboards stuck out of the sand beside them.

Sophia set her board by the towels and immediately hugged both her friends. It made Hannah feel homesick for Linnea and the others back in Michigan. "Taylor! Hi!" Sophia said to one of the girls. Taylor was petite, with short curly hair and flawless skin that glowed golden brown in the sunlight.

Hannah stood behind Sophia, trying to keep the right side of her face hidden. But she couldn't exactly stick her head in the sand and hide. Taylor stepped around Sophia and said, "Hi, I'm Taylor."

"I'm Hannah."

"Obviously!" Taylor's laugh was big, friendly, and contagious. "Sophia told us you were coming."

Hannah wondered what else Sophia had said about her. Even with the baseball cap, Hannah couldn't hide her giant birthmark, which was like a map drawn on her pale skin. Hannah saw the moment Taylor noticed it. Her mouth formed a surprised circle; then she quickly looked down at her pink polished toenails.

Sophia's other friend approached Hannah with a wide, bright smile, her thick brown hair hanging in a braid over her shoulder. She moved with the confidence of someone who played lots of sports. "Hi, Hannah. I'm Jackie."

The moment Jackie noticed the birthmark, her smile got even wider, and she didn't look away. Hannah couldn't help liking her for it, even if she was Sophia's friend.

"Oh yeah, this is Hannah," Sophia said, as if they hadn't already introduced themselves. She turned her back on them to lay out her towel. Jackie gestured to the bare stretch of sand beside a pale green beach blanket. "You can set your stuff down next to mine."

Hannah spread out her towel and looked around. "Do all these kids go to your school?"

Everywhere she looked, it seemed that there were kids her age, surfing, swimming, and boogie boarding. The beach was full of families playing in the sand and people soaking up the sun.

Taylor shrugged. "It's a mix."

Jackie pointed at a group of girls. "They go to our school, but they're a year older than we are, so you probably won't have classes with them." It hit Hannah that it wasn't just their school, it was her school too. She couldn't picture starting sixth grade anywhere except back home with her friends. Jackie pointed at another cluster of kids sitting on some of the giant rocks scattered along the beach. "They don't, but we all went to surfing camp together when we were kids."

The three of them seemed to know everyone on the beach. It made Hannah feel lonely, even though she was surrounded by people. She'd have more fun if Poppy were with her—at least then she'd know someone.

Taylor tipped her chin at a family farther up the sand. A dad and his two sons were stepping into wetsuits. "Brody is in our class. You should watch his dad surf. He's surfed in competitions all over the world and won championships and everything."

"Is that Lacey?" Sophia interrupted. "I thought she twisted her ankle skateboarding."

Taylor and Jackie turned away from Hannah to see where Sophia was looking.

"No, you're thinking about Cassidy," Jackie said. "And she hurt herself rock climbing."

"She didn't twist her ankle," Taylor added. "She sprained her wrist."

Sophia dropped her voice so low that Taylor and Jackie had to lean closer to hear what she was saying. Their eyes went wide, and they nodded and whispered back. Hannah couldn't hear a thing. Not that she knew any of the people they were talking about . . . unless they were talking about her.

"That's bananas!" Taylor said as they all leaned back on their towels again. Hannah resisted the urge to ask what was bananas.

"But I heard Lacey's been working with a surfing coach all summer," Jackie said.

"Really?" Sophia asked. "Is it the same one Amelia used?"

Hannah's head was spinning with all the talk of surfing lessons and competitions and rock climbing. She'd never felt so far from her old life. As she listened to the other girls, it occurred to her that Poppy was definitely a California dog—she had the right adventurous spirit and boundless energy. It was just too bad Hannah wasn't a marathon runner, since it seemed like that would be the only way to tire Poppy out completely.

Jackie turned to Hannah. "You're from Michigan, right? I bet there's no surfing there."

"Not really. It's mostly smaller lakes," Hannah said. "Well, except for the Great Lakes. But I've seen people surfing on Lake Michigan when we've visited the beach."

"The beach? That's not like a real beach, though, right?" Sophia asked.

Hannah shrugged. "There's sand and water. We even get whitecaps."

Hannah didn't mention that she never went in the water when it was that rough, even though she was a good swimmer. And the ocean waves seemed so much more powerful than the waves in the Great Lakes.

Sophia laughed. The other two joined in. It wasn't mean, exactly, but Hannah still felt her face heat up with embarrassment. She picked sand off her towel to keep the right side of her face turned away from the other girls.

"But it snows a lot, right?" Taylor asked. "What do you do all winter?"

"Stay inside," Hannah said. The three California girls stared at her with wide eyes. Hannah smiled. "I'm kidding."

Jackie and Taylor laughed for real. Hannah continued, "I mean, there are some days when it's too freezing to be outside. But there are lots of days when it's not too bad and we go cross-country skiing or skating at the ice rink they make in the park every year."

Taylor shivered. "That all sounds way too cold."

"I don't know," Jackie said. "It sounds kind of fun. Like living in a Christmas movie."

Hannah smiled. It was really beautiful when everything was covered in a sparkling white blanket of snow. Sounds were muffled by the snowflakes, and the whole world felt quiet and peaceful. An entire winter of sunshine and blue skies was going to be so weird.

"I bet Monty would love playing in the snow," Jackie said. She scooped a handful of sand into a little mound beside her blanket, as if she were building a tiny sandcastle or a snowman.

"Who's Monty?" asked Hannah.

Taylor smiled. "That's my puppy. He'd totally love the snow. He'll play anywhere, anytime."

"Mine too," Hannah said.

Taylor's face lit up. "You have a dog?"

"Her name is Poppy."

"It's her *neighbor's* dog," Sophia said. "I told you, remember? They're in training class with me and Louie."

Hannah bit the inside of her cheek. Why did Sophia have to call her out like that?

"I wish I could have a dog," Jackie said. "Even if it was a neighbor's dog to play with."

"You can come over and play with Monty anytime," Taylor said. She turned to Hannah. "Maybe we can get Monty and Poppy together."

Hannah had just opened her mouth to say that Poppy would love to, when Sophia stood abruptly and brushed sand off her legs. "I'm sick of sitting here. Let's catch some waves."

Taylor and Jackie hopped to their feet, and the three of them tucked their boards under their arms and started across the hot sand together. Hannah was left sitting by herself. She picked up the magazine closest to her, even though she had no interest in reading it. She tried not to take it personally, but Sophia knew she didn't have a surfboard and couldn't join them. The other two girls probably always did whatever Sophia wanted.

Jackie glanced over her shoulder. "You sure you don't want to come?" she called back to Hannah. "You can borrow my board?"

Hannah shook her head. "No, thanks. I'd rather just watch."

Jackie shrugged and jogged after Sophia and Taylor.

Hannah flipped through the magazine, not seeing what was on the pages. She wasn't interested in surfing anyway. She didn't care if every person in the whole state of California surfed, it was never going to be her thing.

Hannah watched the three girls paddle out into the waves on their boards. Once they got far enough out, they sat up and dangled their feet in the water, talking and laughing and bobbing up and down as the water gently rose and fell under them. When a bigger wave came toward them, Sophia broke off from the other two and angled her board away from the rising water. After a few strokes, she hopped to her feet and stood up in one smooth motion, skimming the surface. The wave started to crest over the back of her board, but Sophia expertly dipped away from the foaming white water. She rode the swell until it disappeared, her friends cheering her on.

They looked like they were having fun. But all Hannah could think about was that when she'd gone standup paddleboarding with Linnea, she didn't have to worry about sharks or waves bigger than she was. And she hadn't had to worry about anyone making fun of her when she wiped out.

She scanned the beach and watched all the other kids high-fiving each other and doubling over with laughter. Sitting alone in the colorful sea of their towels, Hannah suddenly felt awkward, as if she were on display. She was starting to get hot, and she was pretty sure her sunscreen was starting to wear off, so she grabbed her bag and headed for the boardwalk. She bought a pop—the Midwest girl in her refused to call it a soda—and found a shaded table.

There was a small, shallow tidal pool where families with little kids played in the water and chased one another around the sand. Hannah bet that half of those kids would be asleep in the car before they even made it home. A few people were jogging along the beach. Farther down, she spotted a guy playing Frisbee with his dog. As she sipped her cold drink, she started to get an idea. Everyone at the beach seemed to be doing something active and burning off energy. Why not Poppy?

Romping in the sand and waves was sure to tire Poppy out. And then they could work on the training commands someplace other than Mrs. Gilly's living room, so she'd learn them perfectly. The beach was exactly what Poppy needed.

Hannah tossed her can into a recycling bin and took in the scene around her. She was starting to see the beach in a new light. Now she couldn't wait to come back the next day with Poppy.

★ CHAPTER 9 ★

The next afternoon, Poppy bounced at the end of her leash and tugged Hannah across the sand. The pup's head swung from side to side and her tail was a wagging blur as she tried to take in all the new sights and smells. Once they reached an open stretch of sand that wasn't too crowded, Hannah dropped her bag, peeled off the shorts and T-shirt she had on over her bathing suit, and kicked off her sandals.

"Let's go, Poppy!" Hannah took off, running toward the water with Poppy bounding alongside her. They ran along the edge of the surf, Poppy snapping at the waves as if she could catch them. A big wave rolled in and swept past Hannah's ankles. Poppy dove into it, and as the white foam receded, she shook herself off in a spray of saltwater and sand. Hannah laughed as she shielded her face.

The happy dog crashed back into the water, splashing Hannah's legs. When the next wave went out, Poppy ran after it until she was chest-deep. Soon enough she was swimming—paddling with her paws and holding her nose above the surface, her leash trailing behind her. Hannah followed without stopping to think that she was heading right out into the ocean.

The next wave was bigger and lifted Poppy up. The dog swam toward shore with the wave, just like Hannah had seen the surfers do on their boards, and Hannah bodysurfed after her. Hannah thought she'd be more afraid of the waves, but with Poppy beside her having so much fun, she didn't find them so scary.

They played until they were both panting and exhausted. Then they ran back across the sand to where Hannah had left her things. She took a few sips from her big water bottle and poured some for Poppy into a small plastic cup she'd borrowed from her little brothers. Once Poppy had washed the sand off her tongue, she plopped down in the sand and rolled over.

Hannah knelt in the sand and rubbed the dog's belly. Poppy twisted around like a pretzel to lick Hannah's arm. Grains of sparkling sand clung to Poppy's wet fur.

"You're a mess," Hannah said with a laugh. She'd have to rinse her off in the outdoor shower by the parking lot before they walked back home. But first they had training to do.

And now that Poppy had gotten in her play time, she would be much more focused.

"You ready to work, Poppy?" Hannah took out her pouch of dog treats. As soon as Poppy saw the pouch, she was up like a shot, her eyes locked on Hannah, her brow furrowed, and her ears perked.

★ ★ ★

Hannah studied the dog for a second. Poppy was so intent and calm that it gave her an idea.

It was one thing just trying to get the dog to sit still, but next time in obedience class they were going to work on loose-leash walking, which meant she would have to get Poppy to behave while she was in motion. Poppy was terrible on the leash. She was always straining against her collar, and sometimes she hunched down and leaped forward as if she were trying to win a sled dog race. Hannah dreaded getting dragged around by Poppy in front of everyone. Not to mention that it wasn't safe for Mrs. Gilly to try to walk her if she was going to behave like that.

But maybe . . . Poppy was being so good after playing in the ocean that Hannah wondered if this was a good chance to teach her to stop pulling.

"What do you think, Poppy? Can we work on walking nicely?" Hannah took out a treat and showed it to Poppy.

"This is really important. You can't pull Mrs. Gilly around anymore."

Poppy tipped her head as if she were listening and ready for her lesson.

"Okay, let's do it." Holding the leash firmly, Hannah started walking. Instantly, Poppy forgot all about the treat and bolted to the end of her leash the way she always did, pulling Hannah after her.

That didn't work at all! Hannah stopped in her tracks.

Confused, Poppy turned around and took a step toward Hannah. She sat and then dropped into a down position. Then she popped back into a sit. She was trying so hard to figure out what Hannah wanted. Hannah wished that Poppy understood English—or that *she* spoke dog—so she could explain it to her. But just as she did with the twins, Hannah had to figure out how to show Poppy what she meant.

"I think we need to take it more slowly," Hannah said. "Come here, Poppy."

She held out the treat between her fingers, and Poppy moved closer. She nosed Hannah's hand, but Hannah didn't give her the treat yet. Instead, she dropped her hand by her leg. Poppy's nose followed until she was standing next to Hannah. Hannah tugged gently on the leash and patted Poppy's bottom until the dog spun herself around so they were facing the same direction. With the leash dangling loosely between them and Poppy's cold nose against her fingers, Hannah took three big steps. Poppy stayed next to her, step for step.

"Good girl." Hannah gave Poppy the treat. "That's the idea. See? You don't always have to pull!"

Poppy nudged the treat pouch and sat by Hannah's side.

"Want to try again?" Hannah asked. Poppy tap-danced her front paws in the sand, ready to go.

Hannah held a treat by Poppy's nose and started walking slowly. Poppy stayed close, her nose glued to the treat in Hannah's hand. Hannah took a few more steps, then let Poppy have the treat. They made their way down to the water's edge and tried it again and again, adding in a few more steps each time.

Poppy seemed to be getting the hang of it, but Hannah knew she couldn't walk around with a fistful of treats all the time. Just like Poppy was learning to sit without the promise of a treat, she needed to learn to walk without being lured along.

"I know you can do this, Poppy." Poppy nosed Hannah's empty hand, then looked up at her. Hannah started walking. "That's a good girl. Okay, let's go! Look at you going for a walk!" Poppy wagged her tail the way she always did when Hannah talked to her. She kept her eyes on Hannah and stayed by her side, the leash swinging between them.

"You're the best, Poppy—you got this!" Hannah encouraged the dog as she counted ten steps in her head. It didn't seem like much yet, but she remembered when the twins had started learning to crawl, and she knew that every inch was a big deal. She stopped and gave Poppy a treat from the pouch.

"Yay!" Hannah cheered. She rubbed Poppy's ears. "You're such a smart girl. Maybe you won't pull my arm off anymore."

She turned to head back in the other direction. "Okay, let's see if we can make it fifteen steps this time. Ready? One. Two. Three . . ."

Poppy stayed close to Hannah's leg until she got to six. Then an extra-big wave rolled toward them. Poppy couldn't resist it. She tugged Hannah over and tried to catch the foam of the breaking wave in her mouth. Hannah had been so unprepared that she stumbled after Poppy, almost falling into the water.

"Hey!" Hannah exclaimed. The wave was gone, and Poppy trotted back to Hannah's side, looking proud of herself for chasing it. "Poppy!" Hannah started to scold the dog, but then she stopped and took a deep breath. She reminded herself not to be mad at Poppy for wanting to play. Getting frustrated wouldn't help—in fact, it would just make things harder because Poppy would feel it. "I know the beach is distracting, but we can do this," Hannah said with an exhale. It was a pep talk for both of them. Poppy shifted her eyes, ducked her head, and whined as if she wasn't so certain.

"Trust me. We'll take it slow."

Hannah stayed close to the waves and started over again. She took three steps, then rewarded Poppy. She added three more steps. Her next goal was ten steps, but as she reached five, she noticed another big wave coming toward them. She had a feeling Poppy wouldn't be able to resist it, so she stopped and gave Poppy a treat to distract her before the dog had a chance to be tempted by the wave.

Poppy swallowed the treat, then spun around to snap at the water as it hit the shore. Hannah was ready this time. She braced herself in the sand so Poppy couldn't yank her into the ocean. When Poppy got to the end of her leash, she turned back to Hannah. When Hannah didn't come into the waves with her, Poppy splashed back to Hannah's side. It wasn't as much fun for her if they weren't playing together.

Hannah scratched Poppy under the chin. "That's a good girl! Ready to see if we can make it to those rocks?"

Without waiting for a reply, Hannah took off, walking a little faster this time to keep Poppy's attention. Hannah felt an extra little kick in her step as they walked—a burst of energy from being in sync with Poppy and feeling that they were making some real progress.

"Remember—you don't need to eat all the waves," she said as they trotted across the sand.

After twenty steps, Hannah stopped to give Poppy a treat. A seagull swooped onto the sand a few feet away, and Hannah braced herself. Poppy looked at the bird, but didn't lunge after it. "That's a good pup!" Hannah said, giving Poppy three treats instead of just one. Then she counted off twenty more steps. Then thirty. Poppy trotted alongside her, eyes on Hannah.

Hannah didn't really know what to do next, but she didn't let that stop her. She paid close attention to Poppy, and as long as the dog was tuned in and following along, Hannah figured she'd just keep at it. She knew that Poppy responded to the sound of her voice, so she kept up a steady stream of chatter as they headed down the beach. Hannah didn't even know what she was saying—she was just trying to keep Poppy interested. Sure enough, Poppy seemed to take in her every word as Hannah counted steps out loud and blabbed on about how different the ocean was from the lake back home in Michigan.

Hannah was paying such close attention to Poppy that she didn't notice the seal sitting on one of the rocks ahead of them until it let out a loud, squawking bark. Poppy froze, her ears shot up, and her whole body went taut. Hannah came to a halt too and gaped at the rotund blue-gray creature. She'd never seen a seal outside of an aquarium! She slipped her hand into her pocket to reach for her phone so she could send a picture to Linnea — she'd be so jealous. They definitely didn't have these back home.

But something gave Hannah pause. Poppy. She looked down at the dog, who was still on high alert, her nose wiggling like a rabbit's. Her stiff stance and serious expression told Hannah that Poppy wasn't sure how to feel about the big, barking water dog in front of her.

"Easy, girl," Hannah said soothingly. "It's a friend, not a foe." She pulled her hand from her pocket and reached for the treat pouch instead. She didn't want Poppy pulling them closer and scaring the seal away — or worse, upsetting it.

"Poppy," Hannah said, her voice low and firm. "Sit." After all their hard work on leash manners, *sit* should be an easy command. Poppy hesitated only a second before lowering her rump to the sand.

"Good dog!" Hannah gave her a treat, then held out her hand like a stop sign. "Now just stay there for a second while I take some pictures."

Hannah took a bunch of photos with her phone and

shot a short video of the seal. Poppy sniffed at the air. She still didn't look totally sold on the weird sea critter before her, but at least she didn't go chasing after it. Hannah gave her another treat for being so good, though she knew she shouldn't push her luck. Poppy could decide the seal was a playmate any second now.

Hannah put away her phone and turned around. "Okay, let's go, Poppy!" She tried to sound excited, like whatever was in the opposite direction was even better than this wild animal sunning itself on a rock. With one last long look at the seal, Poppy turned and followed her, the leash staying loose between them. Hannah forgot to count, but she was pretty sure they'd gone at least fifty steps before she stopped.

"You did it!" Hannah cheered, raising her arms in celebration. Poppy danced around her and let out a happy bark. Hannah was so proud of how well-behaved Poppy had been all day, especially in this new environment, and even with a new species to distract her. She couldn't wait to tell Mrs. Gilly. She knelt down and let Poppy lick her face. "You're a superstar," she mumbled between slurps.

"Sweetie—get away from there!" Hannah heard a voice behind her. She turned to see a young mom, her face hidden behind sunglasses and under a big, floppy hat. The woman was steering her child in a wide arc away from Poppy.

"But I want to say hi to the puppy!" The little boy held

out a hand to Poppy. Hannah smiled and was about to talk to him, but she didn't get the chance.

"We don't know that dog. Come on." His mom scowled. "She could be dangerous."

"Oh, it's okay," Hannah said. "She's really sweet."

The boy looked up at his mom hopefully, pleading with his eyes. His mom gave a final shake of her head.

"I'm sure she is," the woman replied to Hannah, though the tone of her voice didn't sound as though she was so sure. "Come on, buddy." She took her son's hand and led him up the beach.

Hannah's stomach tightened, and a tiny current of anger buzzed in her chest. If this mom was trying to protect her son from Poppy, she was wrong. How could people keep acting like Poppy was a mean dog when they didn't even know her? Poppy was so friendly, and they'd worked so hard on her training. At that moment, she was as well-behaved as any other dog on the beach, maybe even better.

Hannah wanted to go over and introduce Poppy and let her cover the boy with kisses. If only the woman met her, she'd see what a sweetheart Poppy was. And Hannah bet that the little boy would love to pet Poppy, as long as he didn't mind slobbery dog slurps.

But even if she told this mom—and all the other parents—how wonderful Poppy was, there was no guarantee they'd listen. And what if they met Poppy and still acted scared of her? Hannah didn't know if she would be able to take it. Because Poppy was a pit bull, they wouldn't even give her a chance.

Plus, Hannah thought with a sinking heart, if they thought *Poppy* looked scary, what would they think about the girl with the big, ugly birthmark on her face?

At least Poppy didn't notice. Hannah bent down to stroke the big brown spot over the dog's eye. It was as soft as velvet. Poppy closed her eyes in bliss at all the extra attention.

"Let's go, Poppy. We'll get you some ice cream to celebrate all your hard work today." Hannah pushed away her uneasy feelings and led Poppy back toward the spot where she'd left her bag. She'd get cookies and cream in a cone for herself and vanilla in a puppy cup. Poppy pranced along, her tail wagging as if anticipating her treat. If ice cream could fix anything, it was the sour taste of judgmental people.

While Poppy sat patiently nearby, Hannah ordered her cone along with a puppy cup. Poppy wagged her tail in excitement as Hannah brought over the ice cream. She scarfed it down in two bites while Hannah laughed and wiped the rainbow sprinkles from Poppy's nose.

On the way home, Poppy walked perfectly on her leash, exhausted from all the playing and training. That gave

Hannah hope. It'd be great if she could tire Poppy out again before obedience class tomorrow. They'd just have to get there early. Slowly but surely, she'd get people to fall in love with Poppy. Who wouldn't love the happiest dog in the world?

★ CHAPTER 10 ★

The next morning, Poppy jumped into the minivan through the open side door. She sniffed around the floor beneath the twins' car seats for crumbs. She found half an animal cracker and scarfed it up faster than the loud vacuums at the car wash ever did.

"Are you done?" Hannah said to Poppy, giggling and poking her in the shoulder. "Time to buckle up." She scooted the dog into the back row of seats and clipped Poppy's collar to the special seat belt Mrs. Gilly had given her. She kissed the dog on the snout before heaving the big sliding door shut and buckling herself into the passenger seat.

Hannah watched through the side window as her mom rushed out of the house and handed Noah off to her dad at the door. Noah's face was scrunched up on the verge of his next crying fit. He'd been crying all morning, even setting

Logan off during breakfast. Hannah felt bad when the twins got so upset, but she could use a break from the screaming. And she was happy that her mom had agreed to drop her and Poppy off at the park early so Poppy would have time to burn off some energy and sniff around the field before training class started.

They had almost made it out of the driveway when the front door opened and her dad ran out, waving Jenny's shin guards in the air. Her mom hit the brakes, rolled down her window, and stuck her hand out for them.

"Jenny forgot these," he said.

"Okay, we'll make a detour." Her mom sighed and passed the shin guards to Hannah.

"Thanks. Have fun at the park, honey," he said to Hannah. He poked his head in the window and kissed her mom on the cheek before racing back inside to the twins.

"I guess we're headed to soccer camp," her mom said, putting the car in reverse, backing up the driveway a couple of feet, and pulling out again, this time headed in the opposite direction of the park. Poppy stumbled when the car started moving and splayed her paws to regain her balance.

"But we'll be late!" Hannah twisted around in her seat, watching their house—and the route to the park—grow smaller in the distance.

"You've got plenty of time before class," her mom said.

"The whole point was to get there early so I can exercise Poppy," Hannah protested. "Why can't you drop us off first?"

"Because Jenny's stuck on the sidelines without her shin guards."

Hannah felt stuck on the sidelines too, always waiting until everyone else was taken care of first. "Then let us out and we'll walk."

"That's silly. You're already in the car." Her mom glanced at Poppy in the rearview mirror. The dog was too excited to sit. She pressed her nose against the window, leaving smudges on the glass as she watched the coffee shops and art galleries of Deerwood pass by. "Don't worry, she'll calm down," Hannah's mom said, pulling one side of her mouth up into a question mark.

"You might as well sit and enjoy the ride, Poppy," Hannah grumbled. In response, Poppy whined at the sight of two dogs walking down the street with their owners.

Jenny was waiting for them in the parking lot at soccer camp. She jogged up to the car as Hannah lowered her window. "Can I say hi to Poppy?" she asked.

"Just for a second," Hannah said. She knew every wasted minute was more park time lost, but she couldn't say no when her sister wanted to give Poppy attention. Jenny slid open the minivan's door, climbed in, and leaned into the back seat. Poppy strained against her seat belt to meet her, her whole back half wiggling with happiness.

Jenny petted the dog's big head and scratched her under the collar. "Be good in school, Poppy," she said. Poppy's tongue whipped out to lick Jenny's face. Jenny laughed and backed out of the van, wiping her cheek on her shoulder. "Ew. Gross."

★ ★ ★

Hannah watched the dashboard clock the whole way from soccer camp to the park. She could still sneak in a few minutes to run around and get some of Poppy's energy out. Every little bit of extra time would help Poppy be more focused in class. Hannah jumped out of the car as soon as it stopped and opened the sliding door to let Poppy out. She was about to take off for a quick lap around the field when her mom called her back.

"Hang on, Hannah." Her mom stood next to the minivan, watching a car pull into the next space. It was Mrs. Lin's Prius. Hannah sighed. She knew what was coming: her mom wanted her to hang out with Sophia before class, as if spending the entire class together wasn't enough. Hannah shifted from one foot to the other as her mom and Mrs. Lin chatted. Poppy really needed to run.

Poppy had been quietly sniffing the grass by the parking

lot, but now, as if she picked up on Hannah's restlessness, she started whining. As soon as Sophia and Louie got out of the car, Poppy tugged Hannah over to them. The dogs greeted each other with twitching noses and wagging tails while Hannah regained her balance.

"Louie, don't get all tangled!" Sophia untwisted the leashes where Louie and Poppy had gotten wrapped around each other.

"That's so cute," Mrs. Lin said, watching the dogs.

"They're adorable," Hannah's mom agreed. Then she turned to Hannah. "Mrs. Lin is going to take you and Poppy home after class so I can get a little work done."

"I could just walk home." Hannah tightened her grip on Poppy's leash. Why was her mom making everything more difficult?

Her mom gave her a pointed look. "Hannah, please don't argue. I just feel better this way. Mrs. Lin will drop you off."

"Fine." Hannah turned away so her hair fell across her cheek. She could feel herself blushing with embarrassment at being scolded in front of Sophia. It wasn't her fault that Jenny and the twins had taken up her mom's whole morning. Hannah's plan had fallen apart, and it just kept getting worse. Now the other dogs and their owners were arriving, and it was too late to let Poppy stretch her legs before class started.

"We better get going," Sophia mumbled. Hannah nodded without looking at her. She and Poppy followed Sophia and Louie over to the training area. The two dogs trotted side by side like old friends. Poppy walked on a loose leash all the way across the field, and when they stopped in the circle, she sat without needing to be asked. Hannah patted Poppy's head. At least something was going right.

"What a good sit," Marcy said, scratching Poppy beneath her chin. Poppy's tail brushed back and forth in the grass, but she didn't try to jump up on the trainer.

"She's doing much better," Hannah said. "I've been taking her out and practicing with her all week."

"Great!" Marcy said. "Then you and Poppy can be the stars today and show everyone how it's done." She smiled at Hannah and walked away to greet the other dogs.

Hannah's mouth went dry. It was one thing to get Poppy to listen when it was just the two of them, but it was another thing entirely to do it while everyone was watching. Hannah could kick herself—why did she have to go and open her mouth to Marcy? Why couldn't she and Poppy just fly under the radar for one day? She wished she were back at home and could start this whole day over again.

Hannah's palms began to sweat as Marcy made her way to the center of the circle. Hannah had to keep switching the leash between her hands to rub her palms on her shorts. Poppy started to pace around her.

"Poppy, come here." Hannah's voice was too thin, but she didn't want to draw any more attention to herself than necessary. Poppy ignored her. Hannah wanted to get Poppy's attention with a bit of hot dog, but as she fumbled in the treat bag, Trixie the terrier came dashing over to Poppy like a wind-up toy gone mad. She hopped up and put her front paws on Poppy's side, then yipped right in the bigger dog's face. Trixie's tail wagged hard — she was ready for fun. Poppy spun around in a half circle and swatted playfully at the little dog.

Carol came racing over, her purse strap across her body, her hands on either side of her face. "Trixie, my love!" she gasped as she picked up her dog quickly, casting a sidelong glance at Poppy. "You need to stay with me. I don't want anything to happen to you!"

Before Hannah could respond, Marcy clapped her hands to get everyone's attention.

"Okay, let's get started!" she said. "First let's review some of the things we've already learned. Hopefully everyone has been practicing at home. Hannah, why don't you and Poppy come and show us the *sit* command."

Hannah's heart thudded in her ears as she walked with Poppy toward the middle of the circle. All eyes—people and dogs—were on them. Hannah swallowed and tried to give herself a pep talk. *Poppy's a pro at sitting,* she told herself. But then another thought wormed its way into her brain: *As long as you don't mess it up.*

So much for the pep talk. Hannah hated feeling this nervous—and it seemed as if she had been feeling that way every day since they'd moved to California. She didn't know which was worse—having to perform in front of the strangers in the class or in front of Sophia. Why hadn't she just told Marcy she didn't want to do this? She'd been so eager to brag about Poppy, and look where it got her.

But it was too late to back out now.

They managed to go only a few steps when Poppy got distracted by all the other dogs. She was so happy to see them, and she just wanted to play. Poppy tugged toward Louie, then toward Sierra, the German shepherd. Hannah had to hold the leash with both hands and lean back so she wouldn't get yanked all over the place.

"No, Poppy." Then Hannah remembered that she wasn't supposed to say "no." She was supposed to show Poppy what she wanted her to do, not just tell her what she didn't want. But how was she supposed to do that if Poppy was acting like Hannah wasn't even there?

Her mind flooded with confusing thoughts, Hannah fumbled for a piece of hot dog and stuck it under Poppy's nose, but Poppy only had eyes for the other dogs. The little terrier barked, and Poppy's tail wagged even faster. Hannah took a step backwards, almost stumbling on the uneven ground. The unexpected movement got Poppy's attention, and she turned back to Hannah as if checking to make sure that she was okay. Hannah was definitely not okay, but at least she finally had Poppy's attention.

"Poppy, sit!" Hannah said, her voice sounding high and strange. The dog looked at her expectantly. She didn't sit. She acted like she'd never heard the word before.

"Poppy, *sit!*" Hannah tried again, unable to keep the exasperation out of her voice this time. As if responding to Hannah's tone, Poppy jumped up on her hind legs, which was pretty much the exact opposite of sitting. To make matters worse, her front leg got tangled in the leash.

Everyone in the class was silent, watching as Hannah unwound the leash from Poppy's leg. "Come on, you know this," Hannah muttered to the dog. After the amazing day they'd had at the beach, it felt as if Poppy were betraying her. Hannah clenched her teeth in frustration.

As soon as Poppy was freed from the leash, she leaped up again and planted her front paws on Hannah's stomach.

Hannah stepped out of the way, but she was so mad she wasn't sure she could get the command out one more time.

"It's okay," Marcy said. Then, to the class, she added, "Dogs need a lot of practice before commands really stick. Even if your dog sits perfectly in your living room, they may respond differently in new situations. That's why you have to practice in lots of different places with different kinds of distractions. Why don't you try using a treat again, Hannah?"

Hannah wished she could disappear into the ground. But she took out another treat and put it by Poppy's nose to lure her into a sit.

"Sit," she said. It came out more like begging than a command.

Poppy danced around, trying to lick the treat out of Hannah's hand. She jumped up and put a paw on Hannah's arm. Hannah had wanted to show off Poppy's good behavior, but it was nowhere to be found. Poppy wasn't listening.

Marcy finally took pity on her. "Why don't we let Poppy take a break. Does someone else want to try?"

Hannah returned to her spot in the circle, her heart pounding as she tried to shake off her anxiety. She couldn't even pay attention to the other dogs, who were taking turns showing off their sits. She didn't want to see that Poppy was the only one who hadn't gotten it on the first try. She looked down at Poppy, who was prancing around on the grass as if she didn't have a care in the world. Hannah couldn't understand what had happened to the sweet, well-behaved dog from the day before.

The lesson moved on to loose-leash walking, and Marcy demonstrated the first steps to teach a dog not to pull. It was exactly what Hannah had done with Poppy at the beach. But now Poppy was sensing Hannah's stress at the other end of the leash, and her big brown eyes looked worried as she nudged Hannah's hand. Instead of walking by Hannah's side, Poppy bowed down, her tail whipping back and forth. She bounced on her front paws, as if she thought Hannah might throw a ball at any second. When no ball materialized, Poppy took the leash in her mouth and started a game of tug of war.

It was almost as if Poppy were trying to make Hannah feel better by playing with her, but it was backfiring. Out of the corner of her eye, Hannah saw Cleo starting to look over at Poppy as her two owners tried to get her attention. And Trixie was completely distracted by Poppy, as usual. Hannah heard Carol saying Trixie's name with more than the usual sharpness in her tone.

Great, Hannah thought. Now Poppy's antics were starting to get the other dogs worked up, too. "Poppy, knock it off!" Hannah hissed. Poppy dropped the leash and gazed up at her, panting. "Can we please just get through the rest of class?" Hannah said to her. All Hannah wanted was for Poppy to quiet down so everyone else could forget about them for the rest of the hour. But Poppy was a puppy—she couldn't just be turned on and off.

The class seemed to last forever. Hannah managed to get Poppy to sit a few times, but she was pretty sure no one else saw it happen. They'd only seen her acting as wild as she had on the first day of class. By the time it was over, Hannah was sweaty and exhausted.

Sophia walked Louie over to Hannah and Poppy, and Hannah braced herself. She didn't know if she could handle Sophia's comments if Poppy acted up again. And what if Poppy misbehaved the whole way home? But instead of pulling on the leash, Poppy rolled on her back and pawed upside down at Louie. If Hannah wasn't so angry and frustrated, she would've thought it was cute.

"I guess she just wants to play all the time," Sophia said. "Louie will run crazy circles around the couch when we're trying to watch TV, but then he just crashes in his bed."

"Poppy sleeps too." Hannah was trying to defend Poppy, but she realized how silly it sounded even before she saw the look on Sophia's face. Of course Poppy *slept*. "I just mean she's not always like this."

Sophia shrugged. She dropped her voice as they started

walking. "Did you see Trixie wrap her leash around her owner's legs? I thought for sure the woman was going to trip and get grass stains all over her white pants. Who wears white pants to the park?"

It was the first time Sophia had actually spoken to Hannah about something other than Poppy. For a second, it took her mind off the class.

"Or to train their dog," Hannah replied.

But then it occurred to her that maybe Sophia was actually still talking about Poppy. Maybe she'd seen how much Poppy had distracted the other dogs. If Carol and Trixie had been standing near them today, Hannah thought, Carol's white pants probably would've wound up covered in Poppy's paw prints. Hannah saw Sophia glance at Poppy and wondered if she was thinking the same thing.

When they got to the parking lot to wait for Mrs. Lin, Sophia asked Louie to sit. He sat. Even though he bounced up after a second, at least he'd listened.

"Poppy, sit," Hannah said. But instead of sitting, Poppy pulled Hannah toward the bench and jumped up onto the seat.

"Off!" Hannah yanked at the leash, but Poppy ignored her, putting her paws on the back of the bench to look out across the park.

"She really doesn't listen," Sophia said, arching an

eyebrow. "Maybe some rescue dogs just can't be rescued after all."

Sophia's words were like a punch in Hannah's gut. She would've liked to tell Sophia she was wrong, but at that moment, she couldn't. Poppy wasn't listening or behaving at all. Every mean comment and look Poppy had ever gotten came rushing back at Hannah, and she was filled with despair.

She'd wanted so badly to prove everyone wrong, to show that Poppy could be well-behaved. Hannah had felt a bloom of hope after leaving the beach yesterday, but now Poppy was back to her old habits. She seemed like an impossible case.

What if Sophia, and everyone else, was right? Poppy was a handful. And Hannah worried that she wasn't a good enough trainer to save her.

CHAPTER 11

"**Come on, Poppy!**" Hannah gave the leash another tug, and Poppy finally spun around and hopped down to the ground. "I'm just going to take her for a quick walk," she said to Sophia.

Hannah led Poppy over to a cluster of trees. When they were far enough away, she took her phone out of her pocket.

Her mom answered on the fifth ring. "Mrs. Lin should be on her way soon," she said.

"Can you come get me instead?" Hannah asked. She knew it was babyish, but she couldn't stand to be around Sophia for one more minute. And after everything that went wrong in training class, she just didn't have the energy to walk all the way home.

"Is something wrong?" her mom asked. Before Hannah could respond, her mom added, "I've got so much work to do, Hannah. Can't you just ride with Sophia like we planned?"

"I really don't want to." Hannah's voice was small. She picked at the rough bark of a tree while Poppy sniffed around the trunk. "Please, Mom?"

Her mom was quiet for a moment. Hannah bit her lip, trying not to cry. Her mom sighed. "All right. But it'll be a little while before we can get there. Your father isn't home yet, and the twins aren't up from their nap."

"That's okay," Hannah said. Anything was better than getting into the car with Sophia after what she had said about Poppy. Her mom agreed to call Mrs. Lin and promised they'd pick up Hannah as soon as possible.

Hannah slipped her phone into her pocket and took a deep breath. She had to swallow the urge to cry before facing Sophia. When she felt a little steadier, she walked Poppy back toward the parking lot. Sophia was sitting on the bench, Louie chewing on a stick at her feet.

"You don't have to give us a ride anymore," Hannah said. Poppy lay down next to Louie and nibbled at the other end of the stick. Louie put one of his big fuzzy puppy paws on Poppy's nose but let her help him chew the stick to mulch.

"Oh." Sophia shifted her gaze from Poppy to Hannah. "How come?"

"My dad is on his way." Hannah wasn't about to admit that he was only coming because she'd asked.

Sophia didn't seem too disappointed or insist that it

would be easier if they carpooled. She looked past Hannah and stood up. Hannah glanced over her shoulder to see Mrs. Lin's car turning into the lot. Relief washed over her. It would've been so awkward to have to stand there with Sophia, waiting for their parents together.

"Okay, well, bye," Hannah said.

"Bye," Sophia said. "Maybe next week Poppy will learn how to sit."

Hannah was too shocked to respond. Sophia's words felt like tiny darts piercing her skin. Why would she say something so unkind? Why was she acting like Poppy didn't know anything? Poppy knew how to sit this week—she even knew how to sit *last week*. Hannah just couldn't get her to do it in front of other people, and apparently that made it okay for everyone to think the worst of both of them.

Hannah slumped on the bench as Sophia and Louie climbed into the car. She hadn't had a chance to run around with Poppy, but she felt so defeated, she just didn't have the energy. Besides, Poppy was happily chewing the stick Louie had abandoned. Maybe she'd worn herself out misbehaving in class.

Poppy shifted position and leaned against Hannah's shins. Hannah appreciated the dog's warmth as the sun passed behind a cloud and the air turned cooler. She wished she'd worn jeans or brought a sweatshirt. Maybe she would've been better off going home with Mrs. Lin. At least that way she could've been in her room, with this miserable day behind her.

Hannah couldn't remember ever feeling this lousy or alone. She thought back to the times she'd been bummed about something and realized that she'd never had the chance to feel this way, because Linnea was always there to cheer her up. Linnea—that's who she needed right then.

Hannah took out her phone, but she couldn't bring herself to unlock it. What if Linnea was busy and couldn't talk? What if she didn't even pick up? Linnea was probably with all their friends at the lake, having a blast. Hannah felt sure they were moving on without her, thousands of miles away, while she was stuck by herself on this lonely park bench.

The minivan pulled into the parking lot, and Hannah got to her feet. "Let's go home, Poppy."

Poppy hopped up with the stick, whittled to half its size, dangling out of the side of her mouth. "The stick stays here." Hannah reached for it, expecting another game of tug of war, but Poppy dropped it, her attention now on the minivan.

Hannah slid open the back door. A very groggy Noah and Logan were strapped into their car seats. Her dad patted the passenger seat. "Sit up here with Poppy. I don't want to leave her back there with the twins."

Tears prickled at Hannah's eyes. Her parents knew that Poppy was with her, so why couldn't her dad leave the twins at home? It felt like everyone else came first and no one cared about her or Poppy.

Hannah climbed into the passenger seat and managed to get the dog to sit on the floor at her feet. She tried to blink back her tears, but as soon as she closed the door, she couldn't hold them in any longer. Hannah covered her face with her hands and cried.

The van came to a sharp halt, and she felt her dad's hand on her back. "Hannah, what's wrong?"

Her thoughts were a jumble, and she couldn't speak for a second. She took a ragged inhale and held back a sob.

"Honey . . . you can tell me." Her dad's voice was so kind and worried—it was the way he sounded when he spoke to Jenny or the boys. But Hannah felt like he hadn't talked to her that way in so long. His concern broke the dam in her heart that had been keeping all her feelings inside since the day they'd moved—and her whole life had been turned upside down.

"Everything is so hard . . ." She started slowly, but once she did, she couldn't stop, and her words spilled out in a rough jumble. "Sophia is mean, and I'm never going to make friends here. Poppy was doing better, but she was terrible in class. I'm never going to get her trained. She won't listen, and I don't know what I'm doing. Mrs. Gilly is going to have to give her back, and it'll be all my fault. Nobody misses me in Michigan. I hate California, and I want to go home!"

Hannah's breath hitched as tears ran down her cheeks. She barely even noticed Poppy licking her elbow.

"Whoa, wait a minute, sweets." Her dad gently moved her hands from her face so he could look at her. "Deep breath." Hannah took a chugging breath and exhaled as smoothly as she could. "Good. Now, let's take these things one at a time," her dad went on. "In no particular order. I know for a fact that Linnea misses you like crazy. Her dad told me it's been really hard for her too. And you had a million friends back home. It's simply not possible that you won't make friends here!" He squeezed her hand. "I know this is hard," he said. "And I know we're asking a lot of you. But you're the same wonderful, smart girl you've always been, and that's all you need to be, whether you're in Michigan or California or on the moon."

"No one else thinks so," Hannah muttered.

"Hey." Her dad shook his head. "Sophia's a little tough —I can see that. But don't let her or her friends get to you. They just don't know you yet."

"They don't want to know me." Hannah sniffled, feeling sorry for herself. "They won't even give me a chance."

"They will. Trust me. They just need a minute, that's

all." Her dad reached over and patted Poppy's head. "And you know this dog already adores you." Poppy licked his hand in agreement. "Plus, I've already seen a big improvement in her."

"Really?" Hannah asked sheepishly.

"Yeah—you can tell by the way she hangs on your every word. She wants to do what you're asking her to do. She's just learning all the new rules around here, the same way you are. I mean, look at her. And to think I was the one who was worried!"

Poppy's head was resting on Hannah's knee, and she was watching Hannah with soft, worried eyes. Hannah gently scratched the dog's forehead. "Then why didn't you want her in the back seat?"

"Look, she's a dog, and you have to pay attention to any dog around babies. But"—her dad smiled and jerked a thumb toward the back of the van—"you've met your brothers, right? They're wicked. I didn't want them pulling on her ears."

Hannah couldn't help but laugh. At the sound of her voice, Poppy put her front paws on the seat and stood up to lick the tears off Hannah's face. Then she wriggled between Hannah and her dad to check out the babies. The twins gurgled at the dog. Poppy's tail whapped against the front seats as she snuffled around the boys, looking for crumbs, and licked at their socked feet. Logan waved his arms, bopping Poppy in the nose with his stuffed animal. Poppy looked surprised, then cracked a smile, wagged her tail, and buried her nose under his tush, sniffing for more dropped Cheerios in his car seat. Logan cackled, which made Noah let out a huge snort. Hannah and her dad laughed at the scene.

"If you and Poppy can handle these two messy babies," her dad said, pulling her in for a hug, "then you can handle anything."

Hannah wiped her tears with the back of her hand and leaned into her dad's chest. He was right. She and Poppy had nothing to feel bad about. They were both learning, and they just needed a little time.

★ CHAPTER 12 ★

Hannah finished putting on her sunblock and checked her reflection one last time to make sure she hadn't left any white smears. She slung her bag over her shoulder and marched into the kitchen. Her mom and Jenny were eating avocado toast while her dad tried to get the twins to eat something that looked like yellow slime.

"I'm taking Poppy to the beach," Hannah announced. She was going to show Sophia that she couldn't treat people —or dogs—the way she'd been treating them.

Her dad's face broke into a huge grin. "That's great, honey. Do you need a ride?"

"No thanks. We don't mind the walk," Hannah said. She might be done with letting Sophia's attitude ruin things, but it couldn't hurt for Poppy to burn off some of her energy before they got there.

"I want to come!" Jenny said, crossing her arms over her chest.

"Next time," their mom said. "You have a playdate today, remember?"

"Oh yeah!" Jenny cried, her complaints instantly forgotten.

"Han, don't forget breakfast." Her dad held out a box of organic whole-grain breakfast bars.

Hannah wrinkled up her nose—even the cereal bars were healthier in California—and grabbed one. As she crossed the driveway between her house and Mrs. Gilly's, she slipped the bar into her bag. She might be determined to face Sophia and her friends, but that didn't mean she wasn't nervous about it. Her stomach was in knots.

Once she had saddled up Poppy and said goodbye to Mrs. Gilly, Hannah paused on the porch to take a few deep breaths. Poppy was carefully studying a squirrel that sat on the railing, looking like it was throwing an eye roll at the dog. Hannah was glad that Poppy was distracted. She didn't want her to catch her nervousness the way she had in obedience class.

After a moment the squirrel darted off, and Hannah and Poppy headed to the beach.

"Good girl," Hannah said. "Good girl."

★ ★ ★

Hannah spotted Sophia right away. She was in the same place where they'd sat a few days ago, ringed by Taylor and Jackie and their surfboards. Hannah marched across the sand toward them, trying to look casual behind her sunglasses. She didn't know whether Poppy sensed Hannah's confidence or was saving her energy to play in the waves, but the dog stayed close, her loose leash swinging between them.

Hannah didn't wait for an invitation. She laid down her striped towel next to Sophia and her friends.

"Hi, Hannah," Taylor said.

"Hey, Hannah," Jackie said.

Sophia nodded in Hannah's direction.

Hannah's heart was racing as she settled on the towel. Poppy nuzzled her, then rolled over looking for belly rubs.

"Is this Poppy?" Taylor asked, her eyes lighting up. "What a cute dog! Can I pet her?"

"Sure!" Hannah was pleased, and a little surprised, that the girls remembered their names.

Taylor almost acted like it was no big deal that Hannah was there. Jackie scooted closer to pet Poppy too. Sophia could've squeezed in, but instead she picked up her phone and turned away, as if she wanted nothing to do with Poppy and Hannah.

Poppy wriggled on her side until she was lying between the girls. Her tail thumped against the blanket, sending a little spray of sand onto their legs. Poppy hooked a paw around Jackie's wrist, as if she was telling her to keep petting.

Jackie laughed. "Well, she's not shy."

"Not at all," Hannah agreed. "She loves everyone."

"Louie is so good when he comes here," Sophia said, looking up from her phone. "He'll just lie in the sand and sun himself."

"Except that time he peed on your surfboard." Jackie giggled, but she stopped when she saw Sophia's scowl.

"He was just a puppy," Sophia said. "I'd had him for, like, a week."

"It was funny!" Jackie tried to save the moment.

Hannah pretended to look for something in her bag so Sophia wouldn't see her smile.

"She's so well-behaved." Taylor scratched beneath Poppy's chin. Poppy grinned in her upside-down position. "My dog would be trying to eat the blanket."

"The other day we saw a seal on the beach," Hannah said. Her voice was steady, even though her heart was pounding as she told the story to these girls. "I thought for sure Poppy would try to play with it, but she just sat by me and watched it." Hannah felt a little twinge of discomfort—she didn't want to sound like she was bragging. But it wasn't like she was making it up. Poppy really had been great with the seal.

Taylor's eyes went wide. "Wow. My dog would lose her mind if she saw a seal."

"Louie never chases seals," Sophia said, shifting on her blanket to face them. "He doesn't even chase rabbits."

Hannah remembered Poppy streaking across the yard after a rabbit the first time Sophia met her. But she thought about what her dad had said, and she wasn't going to let Sophia get to her.

Hannah smiled. "Rabbits are another story. As soon as one hops by, Poppy practically turns into a cartoon dog, her eyes bugging out and smoke coming out of her ears."

Jackie and Taylor laughed. "That's totally my dog!" Taylor said. "Does Poppy know any tricks?"

"Not yet. She's a rescue, so she's still learning the basics." Hannah stole a glance at Sophia, hoping she wouldn't repeat the awful things she'd said about Poppy after training class. But Sophia had picked up a magazine and was flipping through the pages, seemingly uninterested in the conversation.

"My dog is a rescue too," Taylor said. "We adopted Monty over the holidays."

"I can't have a dog, because of my brother's allergies," Jackie said. "But I definitely plan to adopt one from the shelter when I'm older. There are so many dogs that need homes." Jackie nuzzled Poppy's head. "Just like you, Poppy. I bet you'd be a great running buddy, wouldn't you?" Poppy twisted around to lick her chin, and Jackie laughed.

Sophia had abandoned the magazine and was staring out at the waves, her arms wrapped around her knees. Hannah was surprised to see that she was clenching and unclenching her jaw. Was Sophia . . . angry? A weird thought occurred to Hannah, but at first it seemed too ridiculous to be true. Could Sophia be feeling left out because Louie didn't come from a shelter?

Taylor interrupted her thoughts. "What kind of treats does Poppy like?" she asked. "Monty loves anything with peanut butter. Like, don't try to eat a peanut butter sandwich around him or you'll have a dog in your lap."

Hannah turned her attention away from Sophia. "Oh, Poppy will eat pretty much anything. She even acts like her dog food is a treat."

Before Jackie or Taylor could ask another question, Sophia said, "Let's hit the waves. We came here to surf, didn't we?"

Jackie and Taylor glanced at Sophia and then at each other.

"Right," Taylor said. She patted Poppy's head. "We'll be back later. Stay cute."

The girls stood up to gather their boards. Hannah bit her lip. Sophia *knew* she didn't surf. She probably suggested it to stop Hannah from talking to her friends.

"Come with us, Hannah," Jackie said with her wide, friendly smile. "You can borrow my board if you want."

"I'll hold Poppy for you," Taylor offered.

Hannah hesitated. She looked over at Sophia, who wasn't showing any reaction, then down at Poppy, whose eyes glinted with excitement. Hannah was nervous about trying to surf at all, let alone in front of everyone—especially Sophia. But she'd promised herself she wouldn't let Sophia stop her from having fun anymore, so she stood and brushed the sand off her legs. "Okay, but I've never surfed before."

"No problem. We'll help you!" Jackie said.

Hannah and Poppy followed the other girls to the water, where Poppy began chasing the waves as they rolled in. Somehow the swells seemed bigger than they had the other day. Hannah was a strong swimmer, but she didn't know how she'd do if she fell off a surfboard. She looked around for a lifeguard and was relieved to see a man in bright red swim trunks perched in a tall wooden chair a few feet away.

Jackie was already hip-deep in the water, waving her over. Poppy was pouncing on the waves and chasing them back out. "Don't go anywhere," Hannah said to the dog. She wanted to tell Poppy to wish her luck, but Taylor and Sophia were standing nearby.

"I'll keep an eye on her," Taylor said, holding out her hand for the leash.

"I thought we were going surfing," Sophia said.

"In a minute," Taylor said. "I want to stay and watch Hannah first."

"Fine." Sophia set her board in the sand and folded her arms across her chest.

"Thanks," Hannah said to Taylor, handing her the leash and then wading out to Jackie. She could feel Sophia's eyes burning into her back.

"Have you ever stood up on a board?" Jackie asked.

"I went paddleboarding last summer," Hannah said.

"Great! It's the same idea. You've totally got this." In the shallow water, Jackie showed her how to hop up onto the board and balance. She made it look easy and graceful.

Some of Hannah's nervousness washed away. She'd been pretty good at paddleboarding, even better than Linnea. Maybe she *could* do this.

Hannah lay flat on the board; then, on Jackie's cue, she pushed up to her feet.

The board slipped out from under her, and Hannah went crashing into the water.

"It's okay," Jackie said. "It's weird the first time with the waves. Just try to roll with them."

This time Jackie kept her hands on the board to steady it, but as soon as Hannah was on her feet, her legs shook and she had to drop back to her knees or risk falling off again. Poppy barked encouragement from the beach, jumping against her leash like she wanted to swim out to check on Hannah.

Hannah tried again and again, but she just couldn't get the hang of it. After a big wave knocked her off the board—almost sending her into a backflip—she knew it was time to give up. She hated to disappoint Jackie and definitely didn't want to fail in front of Sophia, but she seemed to be a lost cause. And she could tell that Jackie wanted to catch real waves with Sophia and Taylor.

Ready to admit defeat, Hannah wiped the stinging salt-water out of her eyes and waded back to where Jackie stood holding the board.

"Poppy, no!" Taylor cried. Hannah spun around to see Poppy loose in the water, paddling toward her, with Taylor chasing after. "I'm sorry," Taylor shouted to Hannah. "She wanted to get to you and the leash slipped out of my hand."

"It's okay," Hannah called back. Poppy reached her but, to Hannah's surprise, swam right past her toward Jackie, who stood holding the surfboard. Before either of the girls could register what was happening, Poppy scrambled onto the board with a frantic scratching of her nails, her leash flopping in the water behind her.

Then Poppy stood up, her legs wobbling a little and her tail wagging.

"Check her out!" Jackie laughed, her mouth hanging open.

"No way!" Hannah gasped, her own embarrassment forgotten in an instant. Poppy looked like a pro, balancing steadily as the ocean rocked the surfboard.

Taylor and Sophia splashed toward them.

"Seriously, Hannah — um —" Taylor shook her head in astonishment. "Your dog is standing up!"

A wave rolled toward them, and Jackie gave the board a gentle push. Poppy stayed perfectly upright, riding the wave up onto the sand, her tongue hanging out. She leaped off with a happy *woof.*

"Did you see that?" Jackie squealed.

"That was nuts," Taylor said. Even Sophia looked impressed.

"Let's see if she'll do it again!" Jackie said. She splashed toward shore to get her board while Hannah called Poppy back into the water. As soon as Jackie steadied the board, Poppy pulled herself back onto it. Hannah and Jackie grinned at each other as they pushed the surfboard with

Poppy on it deeper into the water, toward the waves. Hannah patted Poppy's wet fur. Somehow the dog always seemed to know when she was feeling upset. And she always tried to make Hannah feel better.

"How about that one?" Hannah pointed at a small but perfectly rounded wave coming toward them, and Jackie nodded. As it rolled into them, Jackie gave the board a gentle push.

"Go, Poppy!" Taylor pumped her fists in the air as Poppy surfed the whole way to shore again. Her ears flapped in the breeze, and she looked totally relaxed as she squinted into the sunlight. When the dog hopped off onto the sand, a loud cheer erupted on the beach. Hannah had been so focused on Poppy that she hadn't noticed how many people had gathered on the beach to watch. Poppy zigzagged through the crowd, shaking off her coat, spraying people with water, and soaking up the attention.

Hannah turned to the other girls and saw that Sophia wasn't standing with Jackie and Taylor in the water anymore. She felt a quick flash of irritation—had Sophia ditched them to go surfing on her own? But then Hannah spotted her on the beach at the edge of the group of spectators, her phone pointed at Poppy.

When the girls got to shore, Sophia jogged up to them and held out her phone. "Check it out."

She replayed the video she'd captured of Poppy surfing, head held high and tongue hanging out. Poppy looked like she'd been surfing her whole life.

"That's awesome," Hannah said.

"I've never seen a dog surf before." Sophia squinted at her screen. "How did she even know how to do that?"

For a split second, Hannah wondered if Sophia was actually asking how a dog who wouldn't even sit could possibly surf. But this time Sophia sounded more amazed than judgmental.

Poppy ran up to Hannah and tap-danced on her front paws, the way she did when she wanted Hannah to throw her toy again. "I think she wants to keep surfing," Hannah said.

A big *whoop* rose up from the crowd when Poppy neared the water's edge. Everyone had their phones out to record the surfing dog. At the sight of all those cameras, Hannah had the urge to hide behind her hair, but that wouldn't work when it was wet. And besides, it was Poppy who was the center of attention, not her. She was proud of her puppy.

"Can I take her out?" Taylor asked.

"Sure." Hannah glanced at Sophia, who stood off to the side. For once she looked unsure of herself. "Why don't you both take her this time?"

"Really?" Sophia seemed surprised. Hannah nodded.

Sophia smiled and headed for the water, back in her element. "Come on, Poppy! Let's catch some waves."

"Go on," Hannah said to the dog. With one more little dance step for Hannah, Poppy took off running, splashing into the water after Sophia. Hannah watched her go, wishing she knew how to be that confident and carefree. Poppy didn't let the haters get her down. It was as if she knew she could win them over—and she was right.

As the girls spent the afternoon taking turns surfing with Poppy, Hannah realized the most amazing thing about the sweet, happy-go-lucky dog: no matter what happened, she always believed in herself.

★ CHAPTER 13 ★

Hannah almost didn't hear the quiet knock at the front door over the sound of both twins crying. But when it came again, a little more insistent this time, Hannah paused the game she was playing on her phone to answer it. She swung open the door and was shocked to see Sophia standing there.

"Hi." Sophia held out a square blue envelope.

"Hi." Hannah noticed that something was different about Sophia. She seemed quiet, or almost . . . shy?

Hannah took the envelope. "What's this?" she asked. It wasn't sealed, but she didn't open it right away.

"An invitation to Louie's party," Sophia said. "You should come. And bring Poppy."

Louie's party? Hannah thought. *Are dog parties really a thing?* But she didn't say that out loud. "Sure," she replied. "We'll be there. Thanks!"

"Okay, bye." With a nod, Sophia turned and headed back

down the street. Hannah shut the door and leaned against it. After all the fun they'd had at the beach with Poppy, maybe she and Sophia were becoming friends after all.

Hannah looked at the envelope in her hand. It was addressed to her and Poppy in neat block letters. The card inside had a border of dog bones with ribbons tied around them.

Please join us Saturday at 1 p.m.
to celebrate Louie's 6-month birthday!
Treats for people and dogs will be served.

Hannah rolled her eyes. It really was a birthday party for Louie. There would probably be a cake and everything. It seemed silly, but of course she and Poppy would go. Poppy would have a blast.

★ ★ ★

Saturday morning was chaotic as usual in Hannah's house. The twins were fussy. Jenny didn't have soccer camp, so all during breakfast she yelled over the babbling babies about everything she wanted to do over the weekend. Her dad got distracted and burned half the French toast.

Hannah couldn't wait to get out of the house. And she had to admit she was excited that she had plans, and that they included Poppy.

She didn't want to be the first to arrive, so she waited until it was almost one o'clock before going next door to pick up Poppy. When she walked into Mrs. Gilly's house, Poppy was wearing a pink bow on her collar.

"She looks so cute," Hannah said. There would be a lot of new people at the party, but who couldn't love a dog with a bow?

"Don't forget this!" Mrs. Gilly handed Hannah a shiny green bag, with a chew toy in the shape of a stuffed lizard peeking out of it.

"I didn't even think about a gift!"

Mrs. Gilly winked. "It *is* a birthday party."

Hannah thanked Mrs. Gilly and headed down the street. Poppy walked nicely on the leash, even though they could hear other dogs barking as they approached Sophia's house. Poppy even seemed to prance a little, as if she felt special with the bow on her collar.

Sophia answered the door. "Poppy's here!" she called over her shoulder.

Hannah stood in the hallway, Poppy's leash tight in her hand. She wasn't sure what she was supposed to do at a dog party.

"You can let her go," Sophia said, as if she were reading Hannah's mind. "She'll be fine running around."

"Are you sure?" Hannah asked. The house seemed so

clean, with pretty vases that could be knocked off end tables and cream-colored carpeting waiting to be stained with muddy paw prints.

"Totally," Sophia said. Louie came running into the front hall and greeted Poppy with his tail wagging furiously. Poppy bowed down to sniff him. As soon as Hannah unclipped the leash, they went thundering into another room.

"This is for Louie." Hannah handed Sophia the gift bag. "Um, happy birthday?"

Sophia peeked into the bag and smiled. "He'll love it!"

Hannah and Sophia followed the dogs to the living room. Streamers hung from the fireplace mantel, and a big HAPPY BIRTHDAY, LOUIE! sign arced across the top. There was a picture on it of Louie wearing a party hat.

There were two other dogs there: another Mini Goldendoodle from the same litter as Louie and a medium-size brown dog with floppy ears. The brown one must have been Taylor's dog, Monty, because Taylor was busy removing a throw pillow from his mouth. Even with four dogs running around, the house seemed so quiet. There weren't any babies screaming, and the adults were calmly sitting around the dining room table. Everyone seemed happy and relaxed.

Sophia introduced Hannah and Poppy to everyone. Jackie and Taylor were there, along with three other girls Hannah hadn't met before. Hannah felt their eyes on her face, taking in her birthmark. She ran a hand through her hair, trying to casually brush it across her cheek. She hadn't thought that coming to the party meant she'd be the new girl all over again. But, she reminded herself, if Sophia, Jackie, and Taylor were starting to get used to her, so would everyone else.

"Hi." Hannah gave the group a little wave.

"I saw Poppy's video!" one of them exclaimed.

"Me too—it's amazing!" said another.

"I want to skip science camp and come to the beach so I can see her do it in person!" said the third.

"What else can she do?" the first girl asked.

"I . . . I don't know," Hannah said. "I just started training her."

"I bet she can learn *all* kinds of tricks," Taylor said. "She could be like a circus dog. Her name could be Poppy the Perfect Pit Bull!"

"Maybe you could train her to give *you* snacks instead of the other way around," Jackie said.

"As long as I don't mind slobbery, half-eaten food," Hannah said. The girls all laughed. Hannah smiled and lifted her chin. She was starting to feel like she could handle this.

They talked about surfing and dogs, and even a little bit about school. Hannah didn't know any of the people they were talking about, but these would be her classmates too, so she tried to follow the conversation. The dogs tumbled around their legs and under the coffee table, wrestling and playing. Hannah was beginning to think that every party should have a pack of happy dogs.

"Let's take the dogs outside," Sophia said. She led the way to the backyard, where the animals could chase one another full speed around the big tree in the middle of the yard. Hannah cringed when the dogs raced through the flower bed, but Sophia didn't seem to mind. Poppy came over to check in with Hannah and get attention from the other girls. She was panting hard from all the play, her mouth open in its big smile. The dogs were clearly having a blast.

Louie flopped down by Sophia's feet. She rumpled his floppy ears. "You getting worn out, birthday boy?" Sophia looked up at her friends and said, "Wait 'til you see the cake I made for him."

She led the girls and the dogs back into the house. In the middle of the sparkling-clean kitchen island was a sky blue cake shaped like a dog bone to match the invitations. Louie's name was inscribed on it in royal blue frosting.

"It's organic pumpkin peanut butter," Sophia said.

"That's for the dogs?" Hannah asked, her eyes wide. It looked good enough for people to eat.

"Trust me, you don't want that. There's no sugar in it." Sophia crossed to the counter on the other side of the kitchen, where there was a tiered cake platter stacked with cupcakes. "These are for us."

The girls followed Sophia over to the cupcakes. They were decorated with perfect little dog faces that looked exactly like Louie.

"Did you make these, too?" one of the girls asked.

"No," Sophia said. "We—" She was interrupted by a crash.

The girls spun around just in time to see a blur of pink, brown, white, and blue. It took a millisecond before Hannah registered, with horror, what she and the others were seeing: Poppy had her front paws up on the counter and was dragging Louie's cake by the edge of the plastic plate it sat on. A bite-shaped chunk was already missing from one end of the bone, and telltale blue crumbs clung to Poppy's face. As the remains of the cake hit the floor with a pronounced *splat*, Poppy scarfed down the rest in a couple of bites.

Hannah froze, her heart in her throat. She couldn't believe what she was seeing. Sticky peanut-butter-colored crumbs and blue frosting flew everywhere, splattering against the clean white cabinets and sticking to the fur of the other dogs, who were running over to lick the floor. Hannah covered her mouth with her hands. She was mortified by the scene — and Poppy was at the center of it all.

The sound of Sophia's scream unfroze Hannah, and she ran over to grab Poppy by the collar. It was slick with frosting, the pink bow crinkled and stained blue. Hannah managed to pull Poppy away from the plate, but it was too late. The cake was gone, except for the messy splotches it had left all over the pristine kitchen.

The girls screamed and gasped. Sophia spun around to face Hannah. "I spent all day making that cake for *my* puppy," she shouted. "And your bad dog ruined everything!"

Mrs. Lin rushed into the kitchen. Her eyes widened at the mess. "What on earth happened in here?"

"I . . . I . . ." Hannah fumbled for an explanation, but she couldn't get the words out. What happened was that Poppy had wrecked the whole party. Everyone was staring at the bad dog and the girl who couldn't control her. Hannah shrank under the heavy, thick blame in the air.

"Poppy *destroyed* Louie's cake!" Sophia cried. "Hannah

Check Out Receipt

Lisle Library District
630.971.1675
www.lislelibrary.org

Tuesday, June 8, 2021 7:32:45 PM
96500

Item: 730391006474203
Title: Dead of night
Call no.: J HUN SURV TGD 2
Due: 6/29/2021

Item: 730391007422524
Title: Poppy
Call no.: J SHO
Due: 6/29/2021

Total items: 2

LLD OPEN HOUSE Wednesday, June 9
@ 7PM Come meet the architects,
talk with staff, see the overview
of the most recent designs! We want
to hear from you about your Library.

wasn't watching her, and she jumped up on the counter and ate the whole thing!"

Hannah's face burned. She knew her birthmark was flaring red. But it was too late to hide behind her hair. She already saw the pity in Mrs. Lin's expression as she took in Hannah's blotchy face.

Mrs. Lin put a hand on Sophia's shoulder. "Sweetie, calm down. It's just a cake. We have dog biscuits in the pantry."

"He gets those boring biscuits every day! This was supposed to be special. Poppy spoiled the whole party!" Sophia pulled away from her mom and glared at Hannah. "I knew it was a mistake to invite you."

The other girls stood back, as if they wanted to fade into the peach-painted walls. No one wanted Sophia to turn her anger on them. No one was going to stand up for Hannah or Poppy. Taylor was brushing crumbs off Monty's fur. Even Jackie wouldn't look at Hannah.

It felt as if there weren't enough oxygen in the kitchen. Hannah was humiliated and ashamed, and completely on her own. She had to get out of there. Her head down, she grabbed Poppy by the collar, and as they rushed past the other girls, she mumbled that she was sorry. She barely remembered picking up Poppy's leash or stumbling through the front door and down the porch steps.

Tears blurred Hannah's vision as she and Poppy ran from Sophia's house. She was crushed. The party had been going so well, right up until the end. She'd felt like she and Poppy were really fitting in. But now there was no way Sophia would accept her.

Ever.

★ CHAPTER 14 ★

Hannah called Mrs. Gilly the next morning to see if she could take Poppy to the park. She didn't want to go to the beach and risk running into Sophia and the others, but Poppy still needed exercise if she had any hope of keeping training on track. They'd go to the park and play, just the two of them, then practice their obedience commands. And together they'd forget yesterday's disaster. Hannah thought that playing with Poppy might be the only thing that could make her feel better.

"She's resting," Mrs. Gilly said. She sounded tired. "We had a really tough night."

Hannah's breath caught in her throat. "Oh no! What happened?"

Hannah hoped that Mrs. Gilly hadn't fallen or hurt herself. If she was having a hard time getting around, she might not be able to wait for Poppy to graduate from obedience class.

"Poppy was up all night," Mrs. Gilly said. "She was quite sick from all that cake."

"But it was a dog cake," Hannah said, as if that changed things.

"It was, but she ate the entire thing. You'd be sick too, wouldn't you?" Mrs. Gilly asked.

"I . . . I guess so." Hannah's voice was hushed by guilt. "Is she okay?"

"She will be. But she needs a break this morning." Mrs. Gilly said goodbye and disconnected. She didn't say when Hannah could see Poppy again, or offer to call her back with updates.

Hannah lay back on her bed. Her stomach churned. She couldn't believe how awful things had gotten in the blink of an eye. She shouldn't have let Poppy run around Sophia's house. She should have known better than to take her to Sophia's party. At the very least, she should have been able to stop Poppy from eating the whole cake.

Hannah felt awful for making sweet Poppy sick. She wanted to see the dog and tell her how sorry she was. She wanted to make sure that she was okay and help her feel better. But Mrs. Gilly had made it clear that Hannah couldn't come over.

A wave of sadness and humiliation washed over Hannah. Even Mrs. Gilly was upset with her—which was bad enough, but it also meant that Hannah couldn't see Poppy. She could hardly blame her neighbor for not letting her near the dog. She had made a mess of everything. Poor Mrs. Gilly could barely walk Poppy, and now she'd been up all night with her because of Hannah.

But what if Mrs. Gilly never let her see the dog again? The thought of it brought hot tears to Hannah's eyes. With all the time they'd been spending together, she had started to think of Poppy as her best friend.

As her own.

But Poppy wasn't hers. She belonged to Mrs. Gilly.

It was all Hannah's fault. She never should have tried to train Poppy in the first place. She never should have tried to make new friends or gone to that ridiculous party. Hannah had made the mistake of opening herself up, and it had all come crashing down around her.

She spent the day locked in her room. Her parents tried to get her to come out for lunch. She said she wasn't hungry. They knocked on her door and asked what was wrong. But Hannah pretended she was sleeping.

Her phone buzzed with a text from Linnea. *How was the party?*

Hannah dropped the phone back on her nightstand

without responding. She couldn't bear to admit what she'd done to Poppy.

The screen lit up a few minutes later with more texts. *Was there cake? Did you and Poppy get to sing happy birthday to the dog?*

Hannah shut off her phone and turned away from it to stare at her bedroom wall. A sharp pang shot through her. Maybe Sophia had been planning for everyone to sing to Louie. Linnea would've found it hilarious. But Hannah didn't think the idea was funny anymore. It was just one more thing she had ruined.

Eventually Hannah dozed off. She woke up late in the afternoon feeling groggy, her thoughts fuzzy. She sat up in bed and looked out the window. As her eyes adjusted to the light, she saw a familiar brown and white dog being walked past her house.

At first Hannah felt relief sweep through her. Poppy must be feeling better if she was out for a walk. But then Hannah realized something that knocked the wind out of her: at the other end of the leash was a girl she'd never seen before.

Hannah sucked in her breath and held it until her chest hurt. She sat frozen in front of the window, heartbroken but unable to look away. Mrs. Gilly had replaced her.

Not only had Hannah blown her chance with Sophia and

her friends, but even Mrs. Gilly was done with her. As she watched the strange girl walk Poppy, Hannah started crying. She had lost her only real friend in California—Poppy.

Through her tears, Hannah saw the dog pull the lanky girl down the street. Poppy jerked forward, and the girl stumbled. Then Poppy changed direction, circling behind the girl, hopping up on her, and getting them both tangled in the leash.

Poppy seemed upset and restless. She wasn't acting anything like herself. She might have stolen Louie's cake, but in the past few weeks with Hannah, Poppy had become well trained on the leash and knew better than to jump all over people. It was clear that she wasn't listening to the girl at all, and the girl didn't know how to handle her.

Hannah wished desperately that she was the one out there holding the leash.

The girl danced around to untangle her legs as Poppy leaped all over her. She was talking to the dog and gently —but unsuccessfully—trying to push Poppy off of her. Hannah shook her head. One of the first things they'd learned in obedience class was to ignore a jumping dog and give them attention only when they had four paws on the ground.

Just when Hannah thought things couldn't get any worse, they did. She heard the girl cry out, and suddenly Poppy was off like a shot, racing down the street at top speed, her leash dragging behind her.

Poppy had broken free.

Hannah jumped off her bed, ran through the house, and, grabbing the bag of dog treats she kept by the front door, raced outside after her dog.

★ CHAPTER 15 ★

Hannah sprinted across the street. In the time it had taken her to wrench open her front door and hit the sidewalk, Poppy had completely disappeared.

"Poppy!" the girl yelled. "Come back here!" Her voice was strained, and her brow was stitched with worry.

But there was no sign of the dog.

"Which way did she go?" Hannah asked. She was too focused on finding Poppy to be mad at this stranger, who had not only taken her place but had also let the dog escape.

"I don't know." Flustered, the girl ran her hands through her short-cropped brown hair, which was laced with streaks of purple. The girl cupped her hands around her mouth to call for Poppy again. When no dog came running, she turned to Hannah. "She was right here, but then she just took off. I don't even know what got her all excited. We were walking along and she was pulling a little, but it was fine. Until *zoom,* she was just . . . gone."

"Where was the last place you saw her?" Hannah asked.

The girl pointed, a dozen bangles and leather bracelets sliding down her wrist. "Right between those houses."

It was the same direction Poppy had run after the rabbit, that first day she got loose and crossed Hannah's yard.

"She's probably headed for the woods," Hannah said. "Come on!"

They took off, cutting through the neighbors' yards, past a swing set and an empty kiddie pool.

The girl chattered the whole time. "If only we had a tracker thing, like in the movies. Maybe we should bug Poppy's collar so we always know where she is. But we can only do that if she comes home. I'm going to be in so much trouble. We *have* to find her."

When they got to the edge of the trees, they both called out for Poppy.

"Should we go into the woods after her?" the girl asked. "I read a book where a guy was able to follow animals by finding bits of fur stuck to branches and stuff. Maybe Poppy left us clues."

Hannah shook her head. "We don't know which direction she went. I think we're going to need more help." She was breathing hard. She wanted to cry again, but she swallowed the sob building in her chest. She wasn't going to let this girl see how upset she was.

"I'm Althea, by the way," the girl said.

"I'm Hannah."

"Oh! You're Hannah!" Althea turned to face her. "Of course! My grandma told me all about you."

"Your grandma?" Hannah asked. She vaguely remembered Mrs. Gilly mentioning that she had a granddaughter who was about her age.

"Yup, Grandma Rose. I'm visiting from Los Angeles." Althea's mouth quirked into a half smile. "I guess that makes Poppy my aunt?"

Under normal circumstances, Hannah would have laughed at the joke. And she would have been pained, wondering what Mrs. Gilly had said about her to her granddaughter, but right then there was no time for any of that. They had to find Poppy.

Althea must have felt that way too. Her smile faded, replaced by guilt and worry. She called out for Poppy again, and Hannah joined her. Their voices echoed into the woods, bouncing off the trees and back to them, fading away into nothing.

When the dog didn't appear, Hannah said, "We'll find her. Let's go back to my house to get my parents and sister. They'll help us look."

With one last look over her shoulder in the direction Poppy had run, Hannah turned and headed home.

"How am I going to tell my grandma that her dog ran off?" Althea sounded as miserable as Hannah felt.

"I don't know." Hannah remembered how upset Mrs. Gilly had been when Poppy had run out the front door, and she'd been gone only a few minutes that time.

Althea walked backwards so she could talk to Hannah as they went. "Maybe we don't have to tell her right away. Maybe we can put together a search team without her noticing. If she has the TV on, she might not hear everyone shouting Poppy's name. By the time her show's over, we'll have Poppy back home safe and sound!"

Althea talked a mile a minute, punctuating her thoughts with excited hand gestures. Hannah had never met someone with so much energy—it was like Althea was solar powered. She seemed to have the whole plan worked out in her head, but Hannah wasn't so sure it would work. As much as she dreaded the thought of facing Mrs. Gilly, they had to come clean.

Althea finally trailed off, and they walked in silence for a minute. "That'll never work," she said with a sigh. "I guess we have to tell her."

"We do," Hannah agreed.

They reached Hannah and Mrs. Gilly's street, and

Hannah began to steel herself for the conversation she was dreading. Her feet felt leaden, but as they got closer and closer to her house, a little brown and white dot on her front porch began to take on a familiar shape. Hannah let out a cry of joy at the amazing sight: there, sitting by her front door, was Poppy.

Hannah sprinted across her yard, and Poppy ran out to meet her. They both fell onto the grass, and instantly Hannah was covered in wet, slobbery dog kisses. Poppy whimpered and wiggled, her whole back end wagging furiously. Hannah felt her heart bursting with love.

Poppy had missed her, too.

After a few minutes of snuggles, Poppy calmed down and rolled over onto her back for belly rubs. As Hannah petted the dog's smooth, pink tummy, a feeling of calm came over her.

She only wanted what was best for Poppy. And if that meant the dog would be taken care of by Althea instead of her, that was okay. She would help Althea learn to do it right — Poppy deserved that.

Hannah stood and picked up Poppy's leash, which was dusty and dingy from her adventure.

"Poppy, sit," Hannah said. Poppy sat. "Good girl. Stay." She gave Poppy the stop-sign signal for *stay*, then turned toward Althea. Poppy watched her, but didn't move.

"She's so calm," Althea whispered, as if talking too loudly might break the spell. "How did you do that?"

"I'll show you," Hannah said. "If you're going to be taking care of her, there's some stuff you need to know." Hannah took a deep breath and thought about all the things she could say about Poppy. She realized she would have to stick to the basics, or she could be talking for hours. "She's gotten really good on the leash," she began, "but sometimes she gets kind of excited. So if she starts to pull, you just have to stop. Once she comes back to you, you can start walking again. You can even ask her to do a few commands to remind her to pay attention to you."

Hannah realized that she was reciting what Marcy had taught them during the obedience class. Even if the last class had been a failure, Hannah had picked up more than just the basics. She had come to *understand* Poppy.

Althea was paying careful attention, almost as if she was taking mental notes.

"Let's go, Poppy!" Hannah said. She started walking, and Poppy trotted alongside her while Althea scrambled to catch up. When, a few steps later, Poppy started tugging on her leash, Hannah stopped and stood perfectly still. Poppy immediately realized what she'd done and doubled back to Hannah. They started walking again, and Poppy stayed by Hannah's side all the way across the yard. When they reached the street, Hannah stopped. Poppy sat next to her without having to be asked.

Hannah held out the leash. "Here, you try."

"Okay." Althea looped the leash around her wrist alongside her bracelets. She ran a hand through her pixie cut and nodded to herself, giving herself a silent pep talk. Then she was ready to go. "Come on, Poppy!"

Poppy gave Hannah a quick glance, and Hannah nodded at her to go. With her approval, Poppy started walking alongside Althea, letting the leash hang loosely between them. When Poppy started veering off toward a tree, pulling the leash taut, Althea stopped in her tracks, just as Hannah had shown her. Poppy turned around and came back to Althea.

"Good! Now you can start walking again," Hannah said. After the third time Althea stopped, Poppy came back and jumped up on her with her front paws.

"Just ignore her if she does that," Hannah said. "Once she's not jumping, you can pet her and keep walking."

Althea listened to everything Hannah said, and within a few minutes the two girls were walking down the street with Poppy strutting along between them.

"Wow, my grandma was right—you're so good with the

dog," Althea said. "You have a gift! Have you seen those obedience competitions? Or those people who have whole routines they do with their dogs? You could totally do that!"

"Oh—no, I don't think so . . ." Hannah trailed off. The confidence she'd felt just a few minutes before, when she'd been teaching Althea, slipped away. Althea seemed to think that Hannah knew a lot more than she really did. But Hannah was no expert—she hadn't known anything about dog training until a few weeks ago. She'd barely known anything about *dogs*. Hannah brushed her hair over her birthmark and stared shyly down at Poppy.

"I'm new to this," Hannah said with a shrug. "We've just been practicing a lot."

"You've never done this before? Then that makes it even more amazing!" Althea exclaimed. "Can you show me more?"

Hannah had to laugh a little at Althea's enthusiasm. "I guess so."

"Awesome." Althea flashed Hannah a warm smile.

They circled back to Mrs. Gilly's house. Hannah paused at the end of the walkway, still unsure if Mrs. Gilly was mad at her about the cake. Althea stopped too, and Poppy sat down beside her, happily panting from her walk.

"I visit every summer," Althea said. "My grandma's great and all, but most of the time it's just us. It'll be way more fun with you here now."

"Oh—okay," Hannah said. She knew it was a silly response, but what else was she supposed to say? How could Althea possibly know that Hannah would be fun? Other kids in the neighborhood certainly wouldn't agree with that —in fact, they'd tell Althea just the opposite.

Althea seemed supercool and friendly, but once she figured out how awful Hannah was, she'd turn on her, just like Sophia had. And Hannah wasn't going to fall for that again.

Althea didn't seem to notice that Hannah wasn't totally onboard. "I can't wait to go surfing," she was saying. "Come with me to the beach tomorrow!"

"Oh, no thanks," Hannah said.

"Oh, come on . . . it'll be so much fun!"

Hannah shook her head. "Surfing really isn't my thing."

Althea wasn't giving up. "I can teach you. It'll be like a trade—you show me how to train Poppy and I'll show you how to surf!"

"I don't think so." Hannah took a step back, ready to retreat into her room again now that Poppy was safe. She was glad she'd gotten to spend a little more time with the dog, but that was all.

Althea looked like she wanted to say more, but seemed to decide not to push it.

"Okay, well, thanks again for helping me with Poppy.

See you later!" She headed up the walkway to Mrs. Gilly's house with a happy, well-behaved dog by her side.

After they'd disappeared through the front door, Hannah turned toward home, telling herself she'd made the right choice by saying no to Althea.

★ CHAPTER 16 ★

When the doorbell rang, Hannah was still wearing the T-shirt she'd slept in and the faded gym class sweatpants from her old school. Her dad had been called into work early, so she'd been dragged out of bed to help her mom with the twins. Logan was flinging oatmeal all over the kitchen while Noah shrieked and giggled, egging his brother on. Everything within a three-foot radius of the table was spattered with food.

"Hannah, could you get that?" her mom asked, wiping a clump of oats off the windowsill.

Hannah was grateful to leave the chaotic breakfast table behind. She tried to run her fingers through her tangled bed head, wondering who could possibly be at the door. It was probably a package for her mom or a canvasser wanting a signature for some political cause. There seemed to be a new one every week. She opened the door and blinked at the bright sunshine framing Althea and Poppy on her porch.

"The waves are perfect today," Althea said, ignoring Hannah's outfit and messy hair. "You have to come with. I won't take no for an answer." Althea glanced down at Poppy sitting beside her. "*We* won't take no for an answer."

Poppy blinked at Hannah with her big puppy eyes. Hannah dropped to her knees, and Poppy wriggled onto her lap with a contented snort. Hannah wrapped her arms around Poppy and buried her face in the dog's warm, soft fur. She smelled like summer and a little bit like kibble. Poppy leaned into her, then squirmed around to lick Hannah's chin. How could Hannah say no to her?

Besides, Hannah realized, now that Althea was here, Mrs. Gilly wouldn't need her to walk Poppy. She would have to take any chance she could get to spend time with the dog—even if that also meant spending time with Althea.

"Okay," Hannah agreed. "I just need to grab my stuff."

She left Althea and Poppy on the porch and hurried to her room, where she quickly changed clothes, put on sunscreen, and grabbed her beach bag. In the kitchen, her mom stood at the sink washing baby dishes. She'd given up on the twins getting more food in their mouths than they got on their clothes. Hannah stayed by the door, just in case Logan was hiding any more oatmeal in his fists.

"Mom, can I go to the beach with Mrs. Gilly's grand-daughter?" Hannah asked.

Her mom glanced at the twins, then back at Hannah, who was all ready to go. Hannah knew her mom wouldn't want to keep her from going out with a potential new friend. But as much as she wanted to spend the day with Poppy, a small part of Hannah wouldn't have minded if her mom said she needed to stay home and baby-sit. At least it would have been an excuse not to hang out with Althea.

Her mom dried her hands on a dishtowel. "Sure," she said, looking frazzled. "Have fun!"

Hannah hesitated for just a second, her baby brothers watching her as if wondering what she'd do next. But Poppy was waiting for her, and that was what mattered most. "Okay, I'll see you later," she said, hoisting her beach bag onto her shoulder, waving at the twins, and heading out the door.

The girls started off on the walk to the beach. Poppy was already a million times more well-behaved with Althea than she had been the day before. Hannah couldn't help feeling a little jealous, wishing she were the one holding the leash. She could practically feel it in her hand.

"You're so lucky you live here," Althea said. "I wish I could surf more often, but we live so much farther from the beach."

Hannah had been so focused on Poppy, she'd almost forgotten. Althea's excitement about surfing. "Wait—where's your board?"

"I'll rent one," Althea said with a shrug. "Not as cool as having my own, but it'll still float."

Hannah liked that Althea didn't care whether renting a surfboard was cool or not—she just wanted to do what she loved. Poppy paused to sniff a mailbox post. While the girls waited for her to finish, Hannah lifted her face toward the sun. It was another perfect day.

"So, what's the story with your face?" Althea asked. "Does it hurt?"

Hannah blinked in surprise. She couldn't remember the last time someone had asked her about her birthmark. Probably in kindergarten, before the other kids were used to her or knew any better.

"It's . . . it's just a birthmark." Hannah turned away and speed-walked ahead of Althea and Poppy. In her rush to get out of the house, she'd forgotten to put her hat on. Not that it mattered. She knew it didn't really hide anything—it was more like a security blanket.

Althea and Poppy jogged to catch up with her. "I'm sorry," Althea said, the strands of her purple hair glinting in the sunlight. "That was probably rude. Sometimes things just fly out of my mouth. I shouldn't have said anything."

No, Hannah thought. She stopped and turned to face Althea. She hadn't expected her to ask about it, but now that she had, Hannah realized she didn't mind. It was nice to have it out in the open, unlike all the times she was dodging uncomfortable stares. Althea was just being honest instead of playing the game where everyone pretends not to see it even when they're looking right at her.

Hannah tucked her hair behind her ears. "No, that's okay. I can tell you about it."

"Only if you want to," Althea said. "I've just never seen anything like it before."

"That's because a lot of kids who have them get treatments to make them lighter," Hannah explained. "So by the time they're our age, you can hardly see it."

"Why didn't you do that?" Althea asked. "Not that you should have—I'm just wondering."

Hannah liked the straightforward way Althea talked to her. She was genuinely curious, but in a respectful way, not a rude one. And she was comfortable with herself, as if she had nothing to hide—and didn't think Hannah did either.

"My parents said they tried the laser treatments when I was a baby," Hannah said. "But they didn't work for me."

"Is it painful?" Althea asked.

"It doesn't feel like anything." Hannah started walking again. Althea and Poppy fell into step beside her. Poppy nudged Hannah's hand and she ran her fingers over the spot on the dog's face. "It's just part of my skin. But it does get dry and burn easily, so I have to use a lot of sunscreen and lotion."

"What's it like? Having it, I mean?"

"I don't know what it's like not having it," Hannah said. "But sometimes people won't really look at me or don't want to talk directly to me. Like they think there's something wrong with me because of it."

"I bet plenty of them have birthmarks, just not in places anyone can stare at them!" Althea said. They both cracked up. No one had ever made Hannah so much as smile about her birthmark, let alone laugh—Althea was definitely the first.

"When I was little, the school sent home a letter to all the parents explaining that it wasn't contagious," Hannah said.

"You're kidding." Althea shook her head. "People actually thought that?"

"Yep. They got over it, though." Hannah looked down at the ground. "It wasn't so bad back home. But I'm still so new here that I guess people aren't used to it."

"Well, you have nothing to be embarrassed about, that's for sure." Althea handed Hannah Poppy's leash, then turned to walk backwards. She considered Hannah's face for a long moment. "I think it's cool. It makes you totally unique and unforgettable." She sighed and spun to face forward again, her brown and purple hair whipping upward in the breeze. "I want to be unforgettable. I'm just so ordinary."

Hannah didn't think Althea was ordinary at all.

★ CHAPTER 17 ★

"**Ready to surf?**" Althea asked, jamming the surfboard from the rental hut into the sand.

"It really didn't go so well last time," Hannah confessed.

Althea grinned. "That's because you didn't have me teaching you!" She laid the board flat on the sand. "Okay, lie down on your stomach."

"Here?" Hannah nervously scanned all the other people on the beach.

"This is how everyone starts. It's easier to practice getting up without the waves." Althea gestured toward the board. Poppy hopped onto it. "See? Poppy isn't embarrassed!"

Hannah rolled her eyes. "That's because she's a natural."

On the way to the beach, she'd shown Althea the video of Poppy surfing. Althea had said she couldn't wait to see Poppy's skills for herself, but she wasn't going to let Hannah off the hook so easily.

"You'll get the hang of it. Come on." Althea nudged Poppy off the board, and Hannah reluctantly stretched out on it.

"Put your hands down like you're doing a pushup. Then slide this foot here." Althea pointed to a spot on the board. "Then the other foot comes up between your hands. Now, stand!"

Hannah felt a little silly as she popped up to a standing position. But once she was up there, she liked the feel of the board beneath her bare feet. She felt steady and confident. "I think I can do this," she said.

"Um, yeah you can—you just did!" Althea made her practice a few more times on land before they took the board to the water. Now that Hannah felt that she'd mastered the transition from lying flat to standing up, she wasn't even nervous as they pushed the board into the rolling surf.

"Leg," Althea commanded as they stood in waist-high water. Hannah lifted her foot up to the surface, and Althea Velcroed the surfboard's strap to Hannah's ankle as she explained the different kinds of waves and how to paddle to catch each one. Althea knew so much about the ocean and surfing—it was pretty amazing that she was an expert at only eleven years old. Poppy splashed into the water after them. As Althea was talking, Poppy scrambled onto the board, her tongue out and her tail wagging.

"You have to wait your turn, cutie," Althea said. She tipped Poppy off the board and into the water, then led her back to the beach. From the sand, she called out to Hannah, "You've got this!"

Hannah lay down on the board and paddled out a little farther to wait for a good wave. She let a few wash past her before she picked one that felt right. She paddled the way Althea had shown her, then started to do a pushup on the board. She was halfway to a crouch when the board rocked beneath her, and suddenly she wasn't sure she could stand all the way. She put her knees on the board, then tried to stand, but she immediately lost her balance and plunked into the water with a splash.

When Hannah surfaced, Althea called out, "Don't try to kneel. Just stand. Trust yourself."

Hannah wiped the water from her eyes, nodded, and paddled back out. Poppy barked happily on the beach, chasing the waves as they crawled up the sand. On her next try, Hannah got her feet under her as the board caught the wave. She looked down to make sure her feet were in the right position before standing up completely . . . and she tipped backwards right off the board. Ouch! The water stung, and salt got into her eyes.

As Hannah popped out of the water, Althea flashed her a thumbs-up, then held her thumb and forefinger an inch apart. *So close!* Poppy wagged her tail and pranced around the sand, cheering Hannah on. Hannah rolled back her shoulders and told herself to try again. With Poppy and Althea cheering her on, anything felt possible.

Once again, Hannah climbed onto the board and paddled toward the waves. She realized that the swells no longer bothered her, and she didn't even mind wiping out. She'd been so afraid of the waves when she first saw them, but it turned out that she'd just needed time to get used to them. And now it seemed like she'd been swimming in the ocean her whole life—like she was comfortable there.

Maybe one day she'd feel that way about her life in California.

★ ★ ★

Hannah popped up over and over again on the board, trying to get her feet in the right place. It would have been easy to give up and decide that she was better off just being a beach bum, but she thought about Poppy and how it took lots of tries before she learned a new command. If Poppy was willing to keep trying until she got it right, so was Hannah.

As the next wave rose toward her, she pictured the spots on the board where Althea had taught her to put her feet. She remembered what it felt like to stand up when the board was on the beach, and she tried to recreate that steady, confident feeling. She reminded herself to keep her knees bent and not to lean over.

Hannah was so focused on the checklist that at first she didn't realize that it had all come together, and she was standing. She was up for a few seconds—long enough to start to relax—before the wave crested over the back of her board and took her down. She let the water carry her and the board to the beach.

"You almost had it that time!" Althea said, her arms in the air. "You just need a better wave. Stay a little farther ahead of it, then pop up. Don't wait too long."

She held out her fist. Hannah bumped it with hers, scratched Poppy behind the ears, and headed back out one more time, the surfboard tucked under her arm.

As Hannah paddled out, she realized that now she could *see* herself surfing. She knew she could do it. She sat up on her board and watched the waves roll toward the beach. One passed by her that felt perfect, but she didn't make the decision to take it in time. She promised herself she wouldn't miss the next one—and she didn't. She paddled hard as it swelled beneath her board, then paddled twice more. In one fluid motion, Hannah stood up, and suddenly she felt an incredible, unfamiliar sensation—somewhere among flying and sailing and riding a roller-coaster.

She was riding the wave!

Her stomach somersaulted, and she felt part bird, part dolphin. It was more than exhilarating. It was magical.

Her board sliced through the water as it carried her toward the beach. She could see Althea cheering, with Poppy leaping around her.

Hannah stood a little taller as she approached the shore . . . and then she tumbled off the board. Grinning, she wiped the water out of her eyes and saw a cluster of people cheering for her on the beach. It wasn't just Althea and Poppy, but a small group that had been watching her try again and again. She pumped her fist in the air and laughed.

Althea splashed toward her. "That was awesome!"

"I want to go again!" Hannah said. She paddled back into the surf. While she waited on her board for a few other surfers to take their turn, she watched the sun sparkling off the waves flowing in from the horizon one after the other. With each one she saw new potential. Beyond the waves, in the distance, Hannah saw a dolphin leap out of the water, then another one — a whole pod playing out there.

Then it was Hannah's turn. She spotted the perfect swell coming toward her and caught it. This time she stayed up, riding the wave until it flattened into water shallow enough for her to hop off the board and land upright. She walked up the sand with the board under her arm. Poppy danced around her and licked the water off her legs, making Hannah laugh.

Althea gave her a high-five. "I knew you could do it! That was major!"

"That," Hannah said, "was incredible. I get why people love this."

Jackie and Taylor pushed through the knot of people watching the surfers.

"We just got here and we heard people saying a newbie was about to catch her first wave," Taylor said. "Then we saw it was you!"

"Congratulations!" Jackie added. "You looked pretty awesome."

"Thanks," Hannah said. At first she was too excited to remember that it was the first time she'd seen or spoken to them since the party. It wasn't until she spotted Sophia hanging back in the crowd, her arms crossed as she watched her friends, that the painful memory of the scene in the kitchen came flooding back.

Hannah started to crumple inside like a wilting flower. But just as her smile began to fall from her face, something Althea said earlier came back to her. It floated through her mind like a refrain from a favorite song: *You have nothing to be embarrassed about.*

Althea was right. She didn't. Poppy had made a mistake,

and Hannah hadn't been fast enough to stop her. That was all.

Hannah raised her head, squared her shoulders, and smiled at the girls—including Sophia. She felt like the queen of the world, and she wasn't going to let them get her down.

★ CHAPTER 18 ★

After Hannah, Althea, and Poppy took turns catching waves, the girls returned the surfboard to the rental hut and went to the boardwalk for ice cream. They licked their dripping cones while watching the other surfers. Hannah's arms and legs were shaking from this new kind of exertion, and she could tell she was going to be sore the next day.

She couldn't help noticing that surfing seemed to come naturally to Sophia and her friends. They were as steady on the water as they were on land. She had to remind herself that they'd been working at it a lot longer than she had.

"You up for a hike?" Althea asked as a stream of bright green pistachio ice cream melted down the side of her cone and dripped onto the asphalt. Poppy quickly licked it up and snarfled the ground, looking for more.

Hannah was up for anything. "Sure!" she said. Tired as she was, she felt energized by the ocean and her success.

Althea nodded toward the far end of the beach, where tall bluffs towered over the sand. "There's a great spot over there that has the best view."

"Let's do it," Hannah said.

Althea gave Poppy the last bite of her cone, then led the way past the boardwalk shops and the families sprawling on beach blankets to a trail that wound up into the hillside. Hannah had never noticed it. If she had, she probably wouldn't have dared to go up it on her own. But Althea was so fearless, it didn't surprise Hannah that she would explore every inch of the coast. Even though Hannah couldn't see where the trail led, she marched toward it. She felt braver around Althea.

As the girls began to make their way up the trail, two men were coming the other way with their dog off leash. The Labrador lumbered over to greet Poppy. The dogs sniffed each other's heads, as if sharing news of their adventures.

"This is Blue's favorite trail," one of the men said. "Your pup's going to have a blast!"

Hannah looked ahead and couldn't see anyone else coming—the trail seemed pretty empty at that time of day. She wanted Poppy to enjoy the trek as much as Blue had. She unclipped the leash, expecting Poppy to jog ahead and at the same time hoping the dog wouldn't run off once she realized she was free. But Poppy just stood watching her, waiting for Hannah's next move.

"Let's go," Hannah said. She and Althea continued up the trail, Poppy at their heels. The wide, sandy path gave the girls plenty of room to walk side by side. The rocky landscape was lush with green coastal scrub. Beyond that, there were sweeping views of the ocean.

For a minute Hannah worried that Poppy might run through the scrub toward the edge of the cliffs, even though the trail wasn't too close to the rim. But Poppy stayed on the path, sniffing at the low shrubs and other plants that lined its edges. She'd trot a few feet ahead and then wait, looking back at the girls as if telling them to hurry up. Or she'd run back to Hannah for a scratch under her collar. She'd stay by Hannah's side until she decided that the girls were walking too slow, then she'd trot ahead to explore. She never strayed far from them.

As they wound their way up the cliff, Althea told Hannah all about the summers she had spent with her Grandma Rose. Mrs. Gilly had been bringing Althea to this beach as long as she could remember.

"She got me my first surf lessons when I was eight," Althea said. "I think she did it mostly to stop me from sneaking off and playing with other people's surfboards on the beach. I'd hop up on any board I saw lying around and pretend like I was riding a wave. Some people weren't amused by some little kid messing around with their boards."

Hannah laughed.

"But even before then," Althea continued, "we'd come down to watch the seals and look for starfish and build sandcastles."

That sounded so nice. Hannah hoped that maybe, once her parents settled into the house and their new work schedules, they'd bring Jenny and the twins down to the beach more often. When she was growing up, she'd loved going to the lake to canoe with her dad and race her friends out to the floating dock. Her siblings wouldn't have that experience, but there was so much they could do at the beach.

"Mrs. Gilly seems really cool," Hannah said.

"She is. And she's always had really cool dogs." Althea bumped Hannah's shoulder. "But I think Poppy is the coolest." Poppy, who was walking just a couple of feet ahead of them, looked up at the sound of her name.

Before Hannah could respond, something rustled in the plants nearby, and the group came to a sudden halt. A small rabbit hopped out from the underbrush. Poppy caught sight of it and tensed up, her ears perked. Hannah felt herself tense up too, knowing full well that Poppy couldn't resist chasing rabbits! She held out a hand toward the dog, calculating whether she'd be able to reach her collar before Poppy shot off after the bunny.

The rabbit seemed surprised to be out in the open and almost face to face with a dog. It scrambled back and forth across the trail a few times before dashing back under the cover of the scrub. Poppy watched the rabbit disappear, then ran over and sniffed the spot where it had been. After a moment she came back to Hannah. Hannah hadn't even had to give her a command.

Hannah bent down and took Poppy's face in her hands. "You are the best," she said, rubbing the dog's chin. Poppy accepted the compliment with a wagging tail and went back to leading the way up the trail. But if there was one rabbit, Hannah knew, there must be others. She started to notice movement in the greenery around her. Birds landing on woody stems, looking for food. Snakes sunning themselves at the edge of the path. But Poppy ignored them all. She just seemed happy to be out exploring with the girls.

A family with two little boys came down the trail toward them. Hannah wasn't sure how they'd react to Poppy, so she called Poppy back to her. Poppy acted perfectly and trotted back, her tail wagging. Hannah and Althea stepped to the side to let the family pass as Poppy sat calmly between them. Her training was working perfectly!

"What a cute dog," the mom said. "I love that spot on her face."

"Can we pet her?" one of the boys asked.

"You need to ask her owner," their dad said. The boys turned their pleading eyes toward Hannah and Althea.

"Sure," Hannah said. "Poppy, want to say hi?"

Poppy glanced up at her as if she were asking permission too. Hannah waved her toward the kids. Poppy approached them, tongue out and tail wagging. She didn't try to jump on them. It probably didn't hurt that they were already at the same level as she was, so she didn't have to try too hard to lick their faces. The boys giggled and patted her head. The parents scratched Poppy's back, and then Poppy returned to her spot between Hannah and Althea.

"Thank you," the dad said.

The boys echoed him. "Thank you! Your dog is so sweet!"

The mom smiled at Poppy and Hannah as they started walking away. "She's such a good dog!"

Hannah beamed and felt a swell of pride. It was true: Poppy *was* a good dog.

"She was so good with those kids," Althea said. "Has she spent a lot of time with your siblings?"

"Only a little bit," Hannah said. "I think she just really likes little kids."

"So what made you decide to train her?" Althea asked.

"I've never done anything like this," Hannah admitted. "But Mrs. Gilly—I mean, your grandma—seemed like she could use the help."

Althea nodded. "She's not quite the same as before her surgery. She used to do everything on her own, and now it's hard for her even to take care of her dog. My mom's been really worried about her, especially with such an active puppy in the house." Althea sighed, twisting her bracelets around her wrist. "I wish we could take Poppy in, but we can't have a dog."

Hannah's heart sank, knowing that the whole family had talked about whether Mrs. Gilly could keep Poppy. Hannah decided she had to forget the humiliation of the last training class and take Poppy back to obedience school. If Poppy was going to have any chance of staying with Mrs. Gilly—and staying in Hannah's and Althea's lives—she had to graduate.

"You should come to our next training class," Hannah said. Althea could tell her mom how much progress Poppy had made. "You'll see how smart Poppy is."

Althea skipped ahead to catch up with Poppy. "I'd love to!"

They passed through a thin stand of trees and reached the top of the trail. The view of the ocean took Hannah's breath away. Hannah, Althea, and Poppy sat on the ground together and looked out over the rocky cliffs. Hannah couldn't believe how vast and beautiful it was. California was full of surprises, and it looked like some of them might turn out to be pretty great.

★ CHAPTER 19 ★

Hannah hoped that the walk to training class would wear Poppy out a little bit. She was feeling pretty good after Poppy's amazing behavior on their hike the day before, but Hannah needed all the help she could get.

"I can't wait to see Poppy in action!" Althea was a few steps ahead of Hannah and Poppy, walking backwards so she could face them. "I bet she's smarter than all the other dogs."

"No pressure or anything," Hannah said, letting out an awkward laugh.

"Don't worry!" Althea said. "I'm just here to cheer you on."

Hannah knew that Althea was trying to make her less nervous, but she still felt a flutter in her stomach. It wasn't about Althea watching the class. If Althea could cheer her on after she wiped out a dozen times on the surfboard,

Hannah knew her friend would support her no matter what happened in class. But this was the final class before graduation day. There wasn't a lot of time for Poppy to get it right. Today was the make-it-or-break-it day.

When they got to the park, Marcy was setting up orange plastic cones in a straight line. She smiled when she saw Hannah and Poppy. "You two ready for class? We're going to play some fun games today."

"We're ready!" Hannah stood a little straighter. Poppy loved games, and Hannah wasn't going to pass on any of her nervousness to Poppy. They could do this!

Jess arrived with Sierra, her German shepherd. She leaned against a tree and took out her phone while Sierra sat regally by her side.

"Oh, wow. Look at that dog," Althea said. "She looks like she should be in a police car or in the movies."

Althea strode over to Jess and asked if she could pet Sierra. Jess nodded and put away her phone. They were too far away for Hannah to hear what they were saying, but Althea chatted with Jess as she stroked Sierra's head. Hannah watched with a mix of awe and admiration. She couldn't imagine just walking up to a stranger like that, especially one as cool as Jess.

"She said Sierra would fail police school because she's the worst guard dog ever," Althea reported back to Hannah.

"Get this: Jess has been teaching Sierra to fetch her keys, and the other day, Sierra brought her keys to the pizza delivery guy. Like she was inviting him to come back and rob them!"

The girls cracked up laughing. Just then, Sophia and Louie walked by.

"Hi, Sophia," Hannah said. As soon as the words were out of her mouth, the birthday party disaster came rushing back to her. Hannah had been so distracted by Althea's story, she'd forgotten that Sophia was mad enough never to speak to her again.

Sophia turned around at her name and looked surprised to see Hannah and Althea. She opened her mouth as if to say hello, but she must have remembered how mad she was, because she snapped her mouth shut and walked away.

Hannah felt the heat of embarrassment creep up her cheeks. This time, she wasn't feeling the rush of riding the waves, so it was harder to ignore the memory of what had happened. Althea looked at her and shrugged, as if to say, *What can you do?* Hannah had told Althea all about Louie's ill-fated birthday party, and Althea had said that Hannah couldn't make Sophia forgive her, which Hannah thought was pretty good advice.

Anyway, for now, Hannah needed to focus on Poppy.

"Let's get started," Marcy said. "Pick a cone and stand by it with your dog."

Althea moved off to the side while Hannah took the cone at the end of the line, beside the terrier, Trixie. Poppy and Trixie wagged their tails at each other in greeting, but Poppy didn't try to get the little dog to play. She seemed to know it was time to work.

"We're going to play some games today," Marcy said. "For the first one, I'll call out a command for you to give your dog. The slowest dog to sit or lie down is out for the round. We'll see who's the fastest."

Hannah faced Poppy. "Ready, girl?"

Poppy grinned up at her.

"Sit!" Marcy called.

"Poppy, sit!" Hannah said. Poppy sat right away.

"Sorry, Cleo," Marcy said. "You're out this round."

Marcy called out *sit* again, then *down*. Now that Hannah knew what was expected from all the commands, she wasn't afraid to give them—and Poppy paid closer attention to her. Maybe something had changed at the beach, maybe the waves and the trail had helped her and Poppy bond in a new way. They seemed more in sync with each other. She believed in Poppy, and in herself.

Every time Poppy made the cut and got to stay in the game, Althea jumped up and down, yelling, "Go, Poppy!" her bracelets jingling and her hair bouncing.

At first Hannah was a little embarrassed by the attention,

but Althea's excitement was contagious, and the other dog owners who'd been eliminated from the round started cheering for the remaining dogs too. Everyone was really getting into it. Then it was just Sierra and Poppy left in the game.

"Down!" Marcy called.

Hannah repeated the command and gave Poppy the hand signal. Poppy dropped onto her belly.

"That was so close," Marcy said. "But Sierra was faster by a hair. Sierra's the winner!"

Hannah rubbed Poppy's ears. She'd done everything Hannah asked, and Hannah didn't want her to feel bad about getting second place. "Good job, Poppy!"

Then Marcy had them line their dogs up next to their cones and put them in a sit-stay. She told them to drop their leashes and walk ten feet away. Louie broke his stay almost right away and dashed after Sophia. Hannah saw Poppy eye the puppy's movement, her muscles twitching with the urge to leap up after him.

"Stay!" Hannah said. Her authoritative voice cut through the distraction of the other dogs. Hannah wasn't thinking about the other people or whether her voice might draw their stares to her face. It was just her and her dog. Poppy's attention snapped back to Hannah, and she settled into her stay. Sophia's cheeks were pink as she walked Louie back to his spot and tried again.

The games got harder and harder. They had to weave around cones with their dogs walking by their sides. The dogs had to pass the other dogs without pulling away to sniff them. The owners had to get their dogs to lie in down-stays for a full two minutes. Hannah kept her head high and her voice strong. And Poppy responded. Poppy was the only dog who did every single exercise without any major mistakes. Althea cheered them on the whole time.

"Excellent class," Marcy said when the hour was up. Poppy plopped down by Hannah's feet, calm and tired out from working so hard to follow every command. Hannah bent down to scratch behind Poppy's ears.

"I'd like to give a special shout-out to Poppy," Marcy announced. "For Most Improved Puppy. Great job with her, Hannah."

Some of the other dog owners clapped. Most of them smiled at Hannah and Poppy. They didn't seem to see Hannah's birthmark or Poppy's breed, just a girl and a good dog.

"As you all know, the next session is our last class," Marcy said. "We'll have a graduation ceremony at the end, followed by a party. Bring your family and friends to celebrate with you."

Hannah wanted to jump for joy. They'd made it! Poppy was going to pass obedience school—and if she behaved as well as she had today, she'd graduate with flying colors.

Hannah couldn't wait to invite Mrs. Gilly to the party. It would be a celebration of Poppy's getting to stay with Mrs. Gilly, too.

Marcy held up her hand. "But before your dogs get their graduation certificate, they need to pass a final test. Each dog will have to go through a series of obstacles and show that they really know their commands. It's going to be a challenge—even harder than what we did today—but I know you all can do it."

Hannah nodded. She knew Poppy could do it too.

Althea ran over and high-fived Hannah. "That was awesome!" She bent down to kiss Poppy's nose. "You're a rock star, Poppy!"

"Thanks for being our cheering section," Hannah said.

"Anytime! Next time I'll bring pompoms and sparklers," Althea joked. At least Hannah hoped she was joking.

"Hey."

Hannah whirled around to find Sophia, Jackie, and Taylor standing behind them. Louie and Poppy sniffed each other and started to wrestle in the grass. Thankfully, it didn't seem that Louie was holding a grudge about his cake.

"Hi," Hannah said, steeling herself, expecting Sophia to remind her how Poppy had ruined everything, and how one good class didn't change that. She didn't want to have another argument, especially not in the middle of the park.

"Poppy did really well today," Sophia said, her voice surprisingly shy.

Hannah couldn't hide her shock at the compliment. "Um, thanks."

"Yeah," Taylor said. "We just caught the end of class when Poppy got Most Improved. That's so cool. Maybe you can help me train Monty?"

"Sure," Hannah said. "I . . . I could do that."

"She's really good at it," Althea piped up. "She taught me how to work with Poppy too."

Jackie flashed her bright smile. "Hi! I've seen you around the beach. I'm Jackie."

"I'm Althea. Hannah's *friend*."

Hannah blushed at the way Althea emphasized *friend*. But it was true: Althea was her first new *human* friend in California.

The other girls introduced themselves. Althea squatted down and clicked her tongue. Louie ran over to her. He leaned into Althea's hand as she scratched his chin.

"And you are . . . ?" Althea asked.

"That's Louie." Sophia gave a small, hesitant smile. "Poppy's friend."

"Then you must be a really good dog too," Althea said.

Sophia broke into a full smile. It seemed as if she was ready to forgive Hannah and Poppy.

"I really am sorry for what happened at Louie's party," Hannah blurted. "Poppy is too." She knew Poppy probably didn't regret eating the cake, but she figured it was okay to fudge the truth a little.

"It's okay," Sophia said. "If Louie were bigger, he probably would've stolen the cake himself."

"Monty, too!" Taylor chimed in. "Poppy just thought of it first."

"Poppy is a genius," Althea said, patting Poppy's side.

"She sure is," Hannah said, her smile wide. It was all because of Poppy that so many amazing things had already happened to her in California. Now she had to make sure that she returned the favor and helped Poppy ace the graduation test next week. And with all these new friends cheering them on, Hannah was sure Poppy would be brilliant.

★ CHAPTER 20 ★

The next morning, Hannah swept into the kitchen, dressed and ready for the beach. She poured a bowl of cereal for herself and even set out a bowl for Jenny, who was running late for soccer camp because she couldn't find clean socks. Her dad was busy feeding the twins, so her mom got up from the table to help Jenny. When they returned to the kitchen, Hannah was busy eating and switching between texting Linnea and texting Althea.

Her mom set a glass of fresh orange juice in front of Hannah. They'd picked the oranges off the tree the night before.

Hannah glanced up from her phone. "Thanks, Mom."

"You're welcome." Her mom sat down in the chair next to her. She reached over and tucked Hannah's hair behind her ear.

Hannah looked up again to find her parents watching her. "What?"

"We're just happy that you seem so happy," her mom said.

"I knew you'd fit in here," her dad added.

"It's not so bad," Hannah admitted, taking a sip of the best orange juice she'd ever tasted. "I'm actually having a pretty great summer."

Hannah was grateful that her parents didn't say, *I told you so.* But she wouldn't have minded too much, because they had been right. She still missed her friends back in Michigan, but California was starting to feel a little bit more like home.

"Why don't you ask Althea if she wants to have a sleepover?" Hannah's mom suggested.

Hannah's face lit up. "Really?"

She hadn't had a sleepover since the twins were born, even in Michigan. Her parents had said they were worried that she and her friends would wake the babies. Things were finally turning around.

"Poppy, too," her mom said. "I'm sure Mrs. Gilly could use a break."

Hannah jumped out of her chair with a squeal and hugged her parents. She ran out of the kitchen to go next door and tell Althea, leaving her half-eaten bowl of cereal behind.

★ ★ ★

Hannah's parents ordered in pizza for the girls and let them eat it in the family room while they watched movies. Jenny kept sneaking into the room to pet Poppy, but Althea didn't seem to mind the interruptions, and Poppy loved the extra attention. She even made funny faces at the twins when her parents carried them through the room, making the babies giggle.

Hannah and Althea microwaved a big bowl of popcorn right before the twins' bedtime. After everyone else had gone to bed, the girls sat with the bowl on the couch between them, whispering about their favorite movies and the different kinds of dogs and other pets their friends had. Linnea's bearded dragon was by far the most exotic, though Althea knew an Irish wolfhound that she swore was taller than she was.

Althea tossed a piece of popcorn to Poppy, who caught it in the air. "I wish my dad wasn't allergic to dogs," Althea said. "It's going to be so hard to leave Poppy tomorrow morning."

"What?" Hannah sat up quickly, nearly knocking the bowl of popcorn onto the floor. "What do you mean *leaving?* You just got here!"

Had she misheard Althea? There was no way her friend was leaving tomorrow.

"I'm only here for the week," Althea said. "Didn't you know?"

"I thought you were here for the rest of the summer!" Hannah protested. School didn't start for another two weeks.

Althea shook her head. "My school starts next week."

"But Poppy's graduation isn't until next week," Hannah said. "You can't stay longer?"

"I wish." Althea patted Poppy's head sadly.

Hannah reached for a piece of popcorn, trying to act as if it wasn't a big deal. But she was too sad to eat. She needed to move around. She got up from the couch, and Poppy followed her.

Hannah didn't want to think about facing the test without Althea there to support her. And even though she'd known that Althea would be going home eventually, it somehow felt worse that she'd have to face school by herself. She'd practically have to start all over again.

"I'm really sorry, Hannah," Althea said. "I thought I'd told you that I was leaving tomorrow."

"It's okay," Hannah said, making her voice sound as bright as possible. Part of her knew that she needed to be confident in herself—and in Poppy—without Althea's help. Hannah told Poppy to sit and stay. She waited a full minute before giving the dog the piece of popcorn and releasing her. Then she walked in a circle around the room, Poppy walking beside her. Hannah felt a little better in the comfortable routine of working with Poppy.

"You have nothing to worry about," Althea said. "You two are going to pass that test with flying colors! Then Poppy will get to stay with my grandma and I can come visit you both all the time."

"Promise?" Hannah asked.

"Promise," Althea said. "I'm only two hours away."

Hannah settled back onto the couch, with Poppy by her feet. She was still sad that Althea would miss Poppy's graduation and that they wouldn't be able to spend the rest of summer hanging out on the beach together. She wished they were going to the same school. But Althea was right. She and Poppy would be okay without her.

When the movie was over, they took Poppy outside one more time, chasing her around the backyard under the moonlight, giggling quietly as Poppy bounded around them. Back inside, they unrolled their sleeping bags on the family room floor. Once the girls crawled into their makeshift beds, Poppy clambered over Hannah and lay down in between them, resting her head on Hannah's stomach and sighing. The dog was warm and cozy against Hannah's legs, and the three of them fell asleep like a big pile of puppies.

★ CHAPTER 21 ★

Hannah's dad was up early, making pancakes for the girls. As soon as they were done eating, Althea had to pack her things. Her mom would be there to pick her up before noon. Hannah and Althea wouldn't be hanging out at the beach and surfing that day. Or eating ice cream cones and saving the last bite for Poppy.

Hannah followed Althea back to Mrs. Gilly's house to help her pack. Clothes were scattered everywhere in the guest bedroom. It looked like Althea's suitcase had exploded. Hannah had no idea how they'd get everything packed in time.

Poppy jumped up on the bed and settled on top of a pair of jeans. She laid her head on her paws, looking sad. She didn't want Althea to go either.

Hannah picked up a T-shirt and started folding it. But then she noticed that Althea was just stuffing things into her suitcase, so she gave up and sat on the bed beside Poppy.

"When will you be back?" she asked.

"Definitely Thanksgiving," Althea said. Hannah couldn't help being disappointed. That was months away! Althea must have been thinking the same thing because she added, "But maybe sooner if my grandma needs help. Or sometimes we come down here for Halloween if my parents can get away from work. Deerwood goes all out. They decorate all the shops along the boardwalk and do a whole haunted house thing at the beach."

"We could be zombie surfers," Hannah said. She could picture the two of them lurching along the boardwalk in cool zombie makeup.

"That would be awesome." Althea tugged her jeans out from under Poppy and added them to her bursting suitcase. "With a zombie surfing dog, of course."

"Obviously." Hannah ruffled Poppy's ears.

The doorbell rang, and Poppy hopped off the bed to race down the hall.

"Oh no, my mom's here!" Althea jammed the last few things into her suitcase, then sat on top of it while Hannah helped her zip it up. Other than the rumpled comforter on the bed, the room was pretty neat without Althea's clothes everywhere. She really was leaving.

Althea introduced Hannah to her mom, who pulled Hannah into a hug.

"I'm so glad you girls had such a good time together," Althea's mom said. "And thank you for helping out my mom. We all really appreciate what you've done with Poppy."

"I'm really happy to help," Hannah replied. "Poppy makes it easy." At the sound of her name, Poppy let out a happy little snort, and they all laughed.

While Althea's mom spent a few minutes with her own mom, the girls lugged Althea's suitcase out to the car. It took both of them to heave it into the trunk. Althea ran her fingers through her colorful hair. "Okay, then."

"I wish you could stay," Hannah said.

"Me too." Althea threw her arms around Hannah in a big hug, and Hannah hugged her right back. Poppy wedged her way between them for a last scratch from Althea.

Althea's mom said her goodbyes to Hannah and Mrs. Gilly and climbed into the driver's seat. Mrs. Gilly, Hannah, and Poppy stepped back as Althea opened the passenger door. But instead of getting in, Althea turned and dropped to her knees, throwing her arms around Poppy's neck. She whispered in Poppy's ear, then gave the dog a kiss on her snout. Poppy licked Althea's cheek.

Althea wrapped her grandma, then Hannah, in one more hug before hopping into the car.

"I want every detail of how the test goes," Althea said

through the open window. "Tell Jenny to record it on your phone. It'll be like I'm there with you!"

"I will," Hannah promised.

"And we'll text every day," Althea said.

Hannah nodded. "Definitely."

Hannah held on to Poppy's collar as the car pulled away. They stayed on the front lawn watching Althea wave out the window until the car turned the corner at the end of the block and disappeared.

★ ★ ★

As the day of the obedience test arrived, Hannah was bummed that her new friend wouldn't be there to cheer her and Poppy on, but she was more determined than ever. And she remembered what Althea had said—she and Poppy *would* pass with flying colors. Then Mrs. Gilly would get to keep Poppy forever, and Hannah would get to see her dog every day. And when Althea came to visit, the three of them would go to the beach to surf and hike together.

There was a soft knock at Hannah's bedroom door.

"Come in," Hannah said.

Her mom stepped into her room. She hardly ever came in without one of the twins or for more than a second, but now she sat on the edge of Hannah's bed. Hannah suspected that her mom felt bad about Althea being gone, but Hannah liked having her to herself for a few minutes.

"Can I help you get ready?" her mom asked.

"I think I've got it," Hannah said.

Her mom picked up Hannah's old stuffed teddy bear and held it in her lap. "Are you nervous?"

Hannah finished rubbing the sunscreen on her nose and turned to face her mom.

"Not even a little," she said as she pulled her hair back into a ponytail. She and Poppy were ready.

Hannah's whole family piled into the minivan to go to the park. Her dad was driving with Mrs. Gilly in the passenger seat, the twins in the middle seats with Hannah's mom, and Hannah, Jenny and Poppy in the back row. The car was pretty squished, but Hannah was happy that everyone would be there to see how amazing Poppy was.

Hannah wasn't the only one who had brought a crowd. All the other students had their cheering squads with them too. Sophia huddled off to the side with her mom, Jackie, and Taylor. Louie parked himself behind Sophia's legs, as if all the extra people made him anxious.

"Welcome, everyone!" Marcy said. "I'm so glad you all could make it. This class worked really hard. I'm proud of how much they've learned."

Hannah scratched Poppy behind the ears, and the dog looked up at her as if the speech were just for them.

"Let's get started!" Marcy said. Everyone lined up with their dogs. Marcy called out random commands, and they had to get their dogs to sit, lie down, or stand. After a few rounds the commands came even faster, but Poppy and Hannah had no trouble keeping up.

Next, the dogs had to lie in a down-stay and remain in place while the people stepped five feet away. Poppy stayed focused on Hannah, as if she knew how important it was for her to pass this test. Hannah glanced over at her family and at Mrs. Gilly. They were all watching her with big smiles. Even the twins seemed to be paying attention. Jenny gave her a thumbs-up from behind the phone, where she was recording the whole thing.

Marcy played a few more games with the basic commands. Cleo, Sierra, and Louie did really well. By now they knew their stuff, although Cleo did roll in the dirt during her down-stay. Only Trixie the terrier had a hard time. She jumped up on her owner, Carol, and when she was supposed to stay while Carol walked in a wide circle around her, she started to run over to Poppy. A very stressed-out-looking Carol had to chase after her and carry her back toward her spot.

The final exercise would definitely be Poppy's biggest challenge. Marcy had set up a little obstacle course of orange cones that they had to weave through, stopping to sit or turn around at different points. To make it even harder, they'd do it one by one, with the other class members waiting alongside the course as an extra distraction. Poppy was so much better than she had been, but she still sometimes had to be reminded not to pull on the leash — especially when she got close to Louie or other dogs she wanted to play with.

Hannah took a deep breath as she stepped up to the starting line. She could feel everyone watching, but as she looked down at Poppy, she didn't feel flushed or shaky. She didn't worry about her birthmark or what anyone was thinking. All she cared about was Poppy. It was time to show everyone what a great dog she was.

"Okay, Poppy, let's go!" Hannah's voice was strong and confident. She and Poppy set off together, weaving in and out of the cones. They paused at the one with the stop sign on it, and Poppy sat automatically. "Good girl!" Hannah said.

They continued on, past the other dogs and the clusters of friends and family. Poppy trotted by Hannah's side. She wasn't even distracted when they walked past Louie or when Noah started to cry. Hannah and Poppy were totally in sync, as if they'd learned to share different facets of their personalities—as if Poppy had gained some of Hannah's calm seriousness and Hannah had gained some of Poppy's happy confidence.

When they crossed the finish line, Hannah's family cheered. She heard Mrs. Gilly shout, "Go, Poppy!" sounding just like Althea. Hannah knelt down to hug Poppy and squeezed her tightly. The dog licked her face in return. Laughing, Hannah wiped her cheek with her sleeve. Mrs. Gilly caught her eye and nodded. She looked as proud as Hannah's parents—but nowhere near as proud as Hannah felt about Poppy. They'd come so far since their first class.

Hannah was in awe of the dog. Somehow, Poppy had known that she needed to learn how to behave in order to keep this amazing life she'd been given. And Poppy had done more than step up to the plate—she had knocked the ball out of the park. Together, Hannah and Poppy had pulled it off.

"We did it!" Hannah buried her face against Poppy's neck so no one would see her eyes tearing up.

It was official—training class was a huge success. And Poppy wasn't going anywhere but home.

★ CHAPTER 22 ★

When Marcy called Poppy's and Hannah's names to accept their graduation certificate, Poppy pranced alongside Hannah, enjoying her special moment. Hannah didn't even mind being in the spotlight for this.

"You've both worked so hard," Marcy said. "Congratulations."

"Thank you," Hannah said. "You're a great teacher."

"So are you," Marcy replied.

Grinning from ear to ear, Hannah handed the certificate to Mrs. Gilly. It was proof that she could keep Poppy.

Mrs. Gilly read it with a smile on her face. Then she handed it back to Hannah. "You should keep it. It's your hard work." She patted Poppy's head. "I've got all the proof I need that she's a good dog." Poppy wagged her tail.

"You need a graduation picture!" Jenny said, waving Hannah's phone. Hannah hoped her sister had remembered to stop the video recording. But she was also sure that Althea would be amused by the play-by-play.

Hannah balanced the graduation cap Marcy had given them on Poppy's big, blocky head. She knelt beside the dog and they both smiled as Jenny and her parents snapped pictures — just like the paparazzi. Poppy tilted her head in her best red-carpet pose. When they were done, Hannah stood up and bumped into Jess, who was taking a photo of her boyfriend with Sierra.

"Congratulations," Hannah said.

"You too," Jess said. "Poppy seems like a really cool dog."

"Thanks! Sierra too." Hannah took her phone back from Jenny and sent the video and graduation photo to Althea: *We passed!*

Althea texted back right away with a heart. *I knew it. Congrats!*

"Time for a class photo!" Marcy called. She ushered everyone from class and their dogs into a group. Hannah wound up next to Sophia. Poppy and Louie pranced around each other, getting their leashes tangled. It seemed as if they knew the test was over and school was out.

"Congratulations," Sophia said. "Poppy did really well on the obstacle course."

"Thanks," Hannah said. "Louie was great too!"

Everyone managed to get their dogs settled down enough

for the photo. Hannah realized after it was taken that she hadn't let her hair out of the ponytail so she could cover her face. But she didn't even mind. She loved the pictures of her and Poppy together.

The group broke apart to drift off into a big celebration. Hannah watched her parents tote the twins back to the car for a diaper change. Hannah and Poppy meandered toward the snack table, which was loaded with cans of flavored sparkling water, star-shaped treats for the dogs, and dog-shaped sugar cookies for the people. And right at the center of the table was a big blue cake in the shape of a dog bone—a perfect recreation of the one Sophia had made for Louie's birthday.

"Sophia!" Hannah spun around and caught the other girl's eye. "Did you make that?"

Sophia nodded and gave her a small smile.

"It's beautiful."

Each dog got a handful of treats, which they devoured with lightning speed. It wasn't time for cake yet, but Trixie, the terrier mix, was already full of food and excited by the commotion. She skittered over to Poppy, ready to play. She let out a series of high-pitched yaps and pitter-pattered on her tiny paws to get Poppy's attention.

Poppy bowed her chest to the ground, her backside sticking up in the air and her tail wagging in wide swoops.

She leaped sideways, her eyes on the little dog and her tongue dangling from her mouth. Trixie jumped after her with another series of yips. Poppy bowed down again and let out a loud *woof.* Trixie stood up on her hind legs and put her front paws on Poppy's shoulder. Poppy rolled onto the ground, and the two dogs began to wrestle.

"Stop it! Stop, Poppy!" Carol, the terrier's owner, shouted. "Trixie, come! That dog is dangerous! That dog is attacking my dog!"

For a second Hannah didn't know what Carol was talking about. She looked around at the other students in the class, trying to read their faces. They looked just as confused as she did, but they were all staring in the same direction: at Poppy.

Poppy and Trixie were rolling on the ground. Trixie had her tiny jaw around Poppy's neck in a playful grip. Her tail was wagging almost as hard as Poppy's.

"But they're just playing—" Hannah protested.

No sooner were the words out of her mouth than Poppy took off running, Trixie hot on her tail. Poppy zigzagged through the crowd. The grownups laughed as they watched the graceful pit bull dart around them while the hyper terrier scrambled after her on her stubby little legs.

Poppy ducked under the snack table, but instead of following her, Trixie took a different route. What happened next was in slow motion: Trixie leaped on top of a cooler full of drinks, then vaulted herself into the air and sailed forward, her legs stretched out in front of her. She landed with a crash on top of the table and skidded across the plastic tablecloth, coming to a screeching halt right on top of the dog cake.

"Trixie!" Carol shrieked.

"No!" Hannah gasped, her hands flying to cover her mouth.

Carol ran to the table and tried to pick Trixie up, but the dog's fur was slippery with frosting. She slid right out of Carol's hands, kicking up a spray of blue icing onto Carol's perfectly pressed blouse. Carol finally got her hands around the terrier and pulled her in close.

"Gah!" Carol cried, looking down at her stained shirt. "Your dog has been nothing but trouble all summer!"

"What do you mean?" Hannah asked in shock. "They were just playing! And Trixie started it."

"How could you even say that?" Carol huffed. "Your dog is a menace."

Around them, the entire group gasped, then went silent, as if the crowd were holding its breath all at once. Hannah felt everyone's eyes on her. Her heart pounded in her chest, and her cheeks burned. She swallowed hard and tried to stay calm.

Mrs. Gilly stepped in. "Don't you talk to Hannah that way," she said. "If you have a problem with Poppy, you can talk to me."

Hannah felt the tightness in her chest loosen slightly. "Poppy, come!" she said, her voice firm but even. Poppy scurried out from under the table, her tail tucked between her legs. She whined and moved to hide behind Hannah. Resting one hand on Poppy's head to comfort her and hurriedly clipping the leash to her collar, Hannah stood up tall and looked Carol right in the eye.

"We're finished here," Carol snapped. "You can take that dangerous dog somewhere else—like to the *pound*." Trixie wriggled her cake-covered body and yelped in Carol's arms, desperate to get down. Carol gripped her tightly.

Marcy ran over, ready to break things up, but Hannah had things under control. She and Poppy had worked too hard this summer—no way was she going to let someone else take that away from them.

"Stop calling my dog *dangerous*," Hannah said slowly, trying not to let her anger show. "Just because she's a pit bull doesn't make her mean. Poppy is the nicest, sweetest puppy I know, and she wasn't doing anything wrong. She was just playing—your dog is the one who jumped on the table."

Poppy leaned against Hannah's legs, and Hannah could feel the pup's chest rising and falling as she panted. Hannah's heart swelled with love for her. She didn't care how many times she had to stand up for Poppy—or for pit bulls. She would keep telling people the truth.

A loud sob broke the tense silence. It was Sophia, who had just run over and was seeing the destruction and chaos for the first time. She stood at the table, her face buried in her hands. Her mom pulled her into a comforting hug, and Jackie and Taylor stood on either side of her, their arms across her shoulders. Louie had his front paws up on the table and was eating the remains of the cake.

"Sophia—" Hannah began. "I'm so sorry this hap—"

"Stop it, Hannah!" Sophia raised her blotchy, tear-streaked face to look at Hannah. "Just leave me alone!"

"Please—I—" Hannah stammered. But there was nothing else to say. She pressed her lips together and stared down at the ground. After all she and Poppy had been through that summer, this was the worst she had felt.

Hannah's mom ran over from the car, Logan perched on her hip. Hannah's dad was right behind her with Noah.

"Is everything okay, Hannah?" her mom asked, keeping one eye on Carol.

At the sight of Hannah's parents, Carol faltered. She raised her chin and shook out her hair. "Just keep that dog away from us," she said, her voice wavering as she clutched

Trixie. Then she turned to Hannah's mom. "You shouldn't let your children be around a dog like that."

"Don't you dare tell me what to do with my children," Hannah's mom warned. "Poppy has become part of our family." Hannah had never heard her mom use that tone with a grownup before — it was the voice she used when someone was in huge trouble. Hannah relaxed her shoulders, knowing that her parents had her back.

With a final harrumph, Carol spun on her heel and stormed off across the grass toward the parking lot. Trixie hung her paws over Carol's shoulder and looked back longingly at Poppy as she was carried away. Then, with one mighty wiggle, she slipped out of Carol's arms and fell to the ground. Barking excitedly, Trixie raced toward Poppy. The pit bull hopped up, ready to play again. She pulled hard on her leash, way overstimulated from all the yelling and shouting — and cake. It wasn't a good combination for any dog, and Hannah knew she needed to get Poppy away from Trixie before things went from very bad to much worse.

"Poppy, please," Hannah whispered. "Not now."

Poppy yanked again. Hannah wrapped the strap a few times around her hand, trying to short-leash the dog. But Poppy pulled even harder — and then there was one sharp tug and the leash went limp in Hannah's hand.

Poppy had slipped out of her collar.

Hannah blinked at the leash and empty collar dangling in her hand. She looked up just in time to see the dog duck away from the crowd and take off across the park with Trixie.

"Poppy!" Hannah shouted. "Poppy, what are you doing? Come!"

Carol went calling after her dog, too. "Trixie, come!"

Finally listening to her owner, Trixie came sulking back. Carol hugged her tightly and immediately fled the scene. But Poppy . . . Poppy was so much faster, and she just kept running. Hannah called the dog's name, even as tears began to prick the corners of her eyes. Poppy always came when Hannah called—except this time. She had too much energy and there had been too much excitement—and Hannah hadn't trained her well enough to handle a situation like this. If only Hannah had trained her to stay calmer.

It wasn't Poppy's fault or Trixie's fault that they'd gotten out of control—it was Hannah's fault. Poppy had probably fed off of Hannah's anxiety, and now Poppy couldn't stop. Hannah felt guilt sitting in the bottom of her stomach like a thousand-pound brick.

Hannah called after Poppy again and again, her voice high and tight with panic. She heard other voices yelling Poppy's name too.

Poppy didn't even look back. Hannah dashed after her,

her heart pounding in her ears. Her breath came in short gasps as she ran harder than she ever had after the brown and white blur in the distance, but with every step Hannah took, Poppy got farther and farther away from her.

The park ended in a hedgerow that separated it from the surrounding neighborhood. Poppy barely broke her stride as she shot like an arrow into the bushes. By the time Hannah squeezed through a gap in the shrubs, the branches scraping at her arms, there was no sign of the dog.

Hannah spun around, looking up one side of the street, then the other, until she was dizzy. Her chest burned. She couldn't breathe. Her whole body was shaking and her arms stung where the bushes had scratched her. But she didn't notice any of that—she cared about one thing only: Poppy was gone.

And Hannah had no idea where to begin looking for her.

The houses that surrounded her all looked the same. The lawns were identical. Poppy could be in any of the yards or even blocks away by now. Hannah had run as fast as she could, but Poppy was still faster.

"Poppy—where are you?" she called out, but the houses stayed quiet. Hannah's voice cracked as she pleaded to the empty street. "Come back—please!"

Her dad and Jenny came running up, but Hannah looked past them, back toward the park, hoping for a glimpse of brown and white fur. She gripped the leash and collar tightly, as if holding them could make Poppy come back. The jingle of the tags brought fresh tears to her eyes.

Hannah couldn't bear the thought of Poppy running off without her collar and tags. After everything she'd been through, Poppy was a lost, stray dog again. She was somewhere out there, scared and alone.

Hannah had to find her.

★ CHAPTER 23 ★

Hannah wrapped her arms around herself to ward off the evening chill. It was getting hard to see in the fading daylight. Her stomach grumbled. By now her mom had probably already finished dinner with Jenny and the twins. She had taken the younger kids and Mrs. Gilly home hours ago, but Hannah had refused to go with them. What if Poppy was nearby? Wouldn't she hear Hannah calling for her?

Hannah couldn't imagine going home without Poppy any more than she could bear the thought of telling Mrs. Gilly she hadn't found her dog yet. Mrs. Gilly had wanted to stay and look for Poppy herself, but her hip was hurting and she was tired out. Marcy and Jess had searched one end of the park while Josh and David combed the other, but eventually they'd had to go home too. Josh and David had promised to print up flyers, and Hannah had texted them her favorite photo of Poppy—riding a surfboard, her eyes shut against the wind—so they could use it.

Now it was just Hannah and her dad marching up and down the neighborhood streets, calling Poppy's name.

"Han—" her dad started.

She knew by the tone of his voice what he was about to say, and she didn't want to hear it.

"—it's time to call it a night," he finished.

Hannah kept walking, her jaw clenched and her eyes raw from crying and straining to see any sign of Poppy. What if she was hiding just around the next corner?

"Come on, Poppy!" she called out, her voice raspy. "It's okay!"

Her dad stepped in front of her, blocking her path, and rested his hands on her shoulders. She was forced to stop moving. "Hannah. It's time to go home."

Hannah ran her fingers over Poppy's empty collar. She felt like a failure. "I can't just leave her out here."

"But you can't stay out all night, either," her dad said, his tone grim. "Let's get some dinner. We'll be back out here again first thing tomorrow, I promise."

Hannah's stomach betrayed her with a loud grumble. Despite the knot of worry tightening in her chest, she knew she didn't have a choice. There was no way her dad would leave her out here alone, and even if he did, she'd never find Poppy in the dark.

★ ★ ★

After a sleepless night on a mattress that felt like it was made of rocks, Hannah was up and dressed before dawn. Without waiting for her dad, she grabbed her hat and a bag of treats and started walking. She'd decided to start the search in her own neighborhood. Wasn't she always hearing stories of dogs finding their way home? Maybe that meant Poppy was close. Even when she ran away from Althea, she'd ended up back on Hannah's steps.

Hannah circled five blocks, softly calling Poppy's name in the sleepy streets, with no luck. She passed Sophia's house, with its dark windows and silent, judgmental façade. The sun came up, and Hannah felt as if it were mocking her with its brightness in this cheery, peaceful neighborhood. She wanted everything to look as gloomy and dark as she felt—she wanted the world to turn as upside down as her life was with Poppy gone.

Her phone dinged. It was Althea texting for an update. Hannah didn't even have the will to reply, and she shoved the phone back in her jeans pocket.

Defeated and hollow, she headed home. She stopped in front of Mrs. Gilly's house and felt a stab of guilt knowing the older woman was alone, waiting for her dog to come home—the dog Hannah had lost. Then Hannah pictured Poppy sitting on the porch, and her regret turned to a throbbing pain in her chest. It was so painful to think about the dog, knowing she might never see her again. But she couldn't think of anything else.

Hannah's mom came outside and handed her a cup of warm tea.

"Marcy called," her mom said. "She's already back at the park. And Josh and David are picking up the flyers at the printer in an hour."

"Did you talk to Mrs. Gilly?"

Her mom nodded. "She's going to stay home by the phone in case someone finds Poppy and scans her microchip."

"Okay." Hannah shivered, and her mom pulled her in close for a hug.

"Your dad is going to watch the kids so we can head over to the animal shelter."

Hannah pulled back to look at her mom. "Wouldn't the shelter have called if she was there?" Hannah asked. She was sure the workers would recognize Poppy, since Mrs. Gilly had adopted her there just a couple of months earlier.

"They get a lot of dogs," her mom said with a gentle shake of her head. "And Poppy doesn't have her tags on.

They told Mrs. Gilly we should come down there to look around. Maybe someone found her and brought her in."

"Let's go." Hannah headed straight for the car, without even going into the house. She waited in the passenger seat, bouncing her leg impatiently while her mom grabbed her keys and wallet. Hannah felt a tiny current of hope wriggling in her chest. Poppy had ended up in the shelter once before, so maybe that's where she was now, just waiting for Hannah to come and claim her.

Her mom finally got in the car and backed out of the driveway. They drove in silence for a few minutes before Hannah spoke.

"Is Mrs. Gilly upset with me?" she asked softly.

Her mom reached over and tucked Hannah's hair behind her ear. "She's so grateful to you for working so hard to bring Poppy home," she said. "And she trusts you to find her. You know Poppy better than anyone. It wasn't your fault this happened, sweetie."

Hannah turned to look out the window, letting her hair fall back across her face. She swallowed a lump in her throat. How could Mrs. Gilly still trust her after she'd lost Poppy? How was this not her fault? She'd been the trainer, the one in control, and now she'd lost a handle on everything.

The shelter was all the way on the other side of town.

They passed the turnoff to the beach, where kids were probably surfing and hiking and playing with their dogs as if it were just another summer day. They drove down Main Street, past the pet store where Mrs. Gilly bought Poppy's food and treats. Everything looked so normal. But Hannah felt like there'd been an earthquake inside her and nothing would ever be the same.

Hannah jumped out of the car as soon as her mom parked in front of the shelter. She marched up to the desk and held out her phone, showing a picture of Poppy. It was another one of her favorites—this one from when they'd gone hiking with Althea, with the ocean in the background and a big smile on Poppy's face.

"Hi. I'm hoping my dog is here," Hannah said to the young man behind the desk. "Her name is Poppy, and she was adopted here not too long ago. She's a brown and white pit bull and she's really friendly and really smart."

Hannah stopped to catch her breath. The man leaned forward to take a closer look at the picture. He had floppy blond hair and round, worried brown eyes. He reminded Hannah of Louie.

"It's hard to say," he said. "We get a lot of pit bulls. Why don't you fill out this form and then I can show you the kennels?"

He pushed a pink form across the counter with the words

LOST DOG in all caps across the top. Hannah reached for a pen, but it seemed like the form had a million boxes to fill out. It would take forever, and Poppy could be back there in the kennels, terrified and wondering when Hannah was going to come and take her home.

"Please, can't I just take a look?" Hannah pleaded.

The shelter employee looked up and noticed her birthmark for the first time. Hannah watched as his puppy-dog eyes filled with sadness for the girl with the stained face and lost dog. For once, Hannah didn't care—if his pity helped her find Poppy faster, she'd take it.

"I'm sorry," he said. "I really am. But I'm not allowed—"

Hannah's mom stepped up to the counter and rested a hand on Hannah's shoulder. "I believe you already have this form," she said to the man. "Rose Gilly called in all the information this morning."

"I'll check," he said. He disappeared into an office and returned a minute later holding a pink form. "Found it! Okay, let's go take a look."

As he came around the desk, Hannah's mom squeezed her shoulder. Hannah knew she shouldn't get her hopes up, but she couldn't stop the little bubbles of anticipation from rising inside of her. They followed the man down a long hallway and through a door marked STRAY DOG KENNEL.

As soon as they stepped inside, Hannah was knocked

back on her heels by the sound. A riotous, ringing barking erupted from the dozens of kennels lining both sides of the room. It was deafening and disorienting. Hannah covered her ears and knew there was no way Poppy would even hear her if she tried to call out her name. She would just have to look in every single kennel.

Hannah walked quickly down the aisle. She passed gray and white pit bulls with rounded bellies, pointy-nosed shepherd mixes who looked like professors, and cute tan-colored mutts concocted from the best of many breeds at once. She passed a pair of tiny Chihuahuas cuddling in one kennel and a speckled, sad-eyed dog bigger than she was.

None of the dogs looked even a little bit like Poppy. Hannah's bubbles of hope started to pop with each kennel she passed.

"Is this your dog?" the shelter employee shouted, to be heard over the barking. He had stopped in front of the last kennel at the far end of the aisle. From where she stood, Hannah could just make out the burly shoulder of a medium-size brown and white dog leaning against the cage door. She couldn't see the dog's whole face, but she could tell that its tongue was dangling from a mouth parted in a big, familiar smile.

She raced down the row of kennels. The dogs jumped

and barked even louder as she passed, sharing her excitement. As she got closer, she could see the dog's whole body wriggling as it wagged its tail—just like Poppy. Though the dog's blocky head was turned away, Hannah thought she caught a glimpse of cowlike patches on its side, and her heart thunked harder in her chest.

She skidded to a stop in front of the kennel. Words were already forming in her mouth—she couldn't wait to tell Poppy how sorry she was and how much everyone missed her.

But when the dog turned its head, Hannah felt as though someone had punctured her with a needle, and she deflated.

The words caught in her throat, and she stifled a sob.

When she was able to speak again, Hannah said simply, "It's not her."

"Are you sure?" the shelter employee asked. "She looks just like the description that was called in, and sometimes dogs can seem a little different in the kennel than they do at home. You'd be surprised how many people don't recognize their own dogs at first."

Hannah shook her head and turned to walk away with heavy steps. He was wrong. She'd know Poppy anywhere. And that dog wasn't even close. Her face was all white, which meant she was missing the most important thing: the patch of light brown shaped like a birthmark.

Hannah pulled the car door shut behind her, and now she couldn't hold back her tears. As her mom rubbed her back, she sobbed and sobbed, her face buried in her hands. She thought she might never stop crying.

"Your dad is going to search near the park again after he drops Jenny off," her mom said. "We'll find her, Hannah. We will." She knew her mom meant well and wanted to find Poppy too, but somehow her promise felt empty—making Hannah cry harder. She couldn't have responded even if she wanted to. She'd let herself hope that Poppy might be at the shelter, and her disappointment hung like a suffocating blanket over everything.

What was the point? Why bother searching when no one really knew what to do or where to go? Maybe, Hannah thought, she should just face reality: Poppy was gone, and she might not be coming back.

When they got home, Hannah slumped straight to her room. She closed the door firmly behind her, just wanting to be left alone, and crawled into bed.

Sometime later—Hannah had no idea if it was minutes or hours—Jenny knocked on her door. "You missed lunch," her little sister said.

"I'm not hungry." Hannah didn't think she'd ever be hungry again.

"Mom made your favorite grilled cheese with tomatoes."

Jenny set down a plate with a steaming sandwich and a teetering pile of cookies on Hannah's desk. "I added the cookies."

"Thanks." Hannah's voice was dull.

Her sister's face fell. Hannah knew that Jenny was just trying to cheer her up, but nothing except Poppy could do that.

"I hope Poppy comes home soon," Jenny said. "I love her."

"Me too." Hannah rolled over, turning her back on her sister.

★ ★ ★

Once the twins were down for their nap, Hannah's parents came to her room. They eyed Hannah's untouched plate of food.

"You should really try to eat something." Her dad picked up a triangle of sandwich to offer it to Hannah. The cold, congealed cheese stuck to the plate. He set it down again. "Do you want me to make you something else? We've got pasta or pancakes . . ."

Hannah sat up to face them. Her face crumpled into tears again. "What's Poppy going to eat?" she asked. Poppy was used to a full bowl of food and a soft bed. She was probably thirsty from all that running. Hannah shivered at the thought of the dog out on her own for another night, hungry, cold, and scared. "What will happen to her?"

"Dogs are smart," her dad said. "Especially Poppy. I bet she's found a safe spot to curl up in until we can find her and bring her back." Her dad pulled Hannah in for a hug. "She'll be okay."

Hannah pushed him away. "You don't know that."

"I believe in Poppy," he said. "She'll find her way."

Hannah had believed in Poppy too—and in herself. But now that Poppy was gone, Hannah wasn't so sure about anything. She had also lost her way.

"What if she doesn't?" she asked her parents pleadingly. "What if we never find her?"

"Oh, sweetie," her mom said.

"Don't say that," her dad said gently. He lowered himself into her desk chair so he could look her in the eye. "We'll keep looking. Every day. As long as it takes."

Her mom sat next to her on the bed and opened her laptop. "I found some neighborhood sites where we can post photos of Poppy, so people can help look for her. Josh and David papered the town with flyers today, and later we can print up some Lost Dog posters and put them up, okay?"

Anger suddenly flared up in Hannah. She didn't want to make posters. She wanted her dog. She had wasted half the day inside when she should have been out looking.

Hannah snatched up her phone and Poppy's leash and

collar and got up from her bed. Her legs were wobbly and her head hurt from all the crying, but she couldn't stay in her room.

"Hannah, did you hear what I said?" her mom asked.

"Yes," Hannah snapped. She started to storm out of her room, but her dad stopped her.

"Han, come back here."

Hannah turned around in the doorway, but she didn't move any closer. She stood with her arms crossed, her fist clenched around the leash.

"We know you're upset," her dad said. "We're worried about Poppy too."

"You never cared about Poppy!" Hannah cried.

"That's not true," her mom said. "We're trying to help you find her."

"It's too late! Why didn't you help me before she got lost?" Hannah's throat tightened and she swallowed the lump in it. She knew she was being unreasonable, but she couldn't stop the horrible, churning mess of her feelings from spilling out.

Her mom gently closed the laptop. "Hannah, you're not being fair. We couldn't have prevented what happened to Poppy. It was an accident. She got scared and ran off."

"It wasn't an accident." A tear slipped down Hannah's

cheek. She swiped it away with the back of her hand. "It was *my* fault. If I'd never taken her to class, this wouldn't have happened."

"Whoa, slow down." Her dad held out both hands in front of him. "If you'd never taken her to class, Mrs. Gilly would have had to take her back to the shelter. And you and Poppy never would have had such a fun summer."

"Look where it got me!" Hannah shouted. Her parents winced, casting a glance toward the twins' bedroom. Hannah was so upset, she was shaking, but she tried to lower her voice. "I put myself out there, like you wanted me to. I made friends, but now they're all gone. I tried to help Poppy. I really cared about her, but it only hurts more. Now I'm stuck in California and I'll probably never see her again."

Her mom got up, walked over, and wrapped her arms around Hannah. Hannah leaned into her mom and let the tears come.

"I'm so sorry," her mom said, rubbing small circles on her back as Hannah sniffled into her T-shirt. "We've been so distracted since we moved here, but we thought you'd turned things around. This move wasn't easy, and we've been so impressed with the amazing job you've done adjusting to this"—she waved an arm in the air—"this new life."

Her mom lifted Hannah's chin and wiped the tears off her face. She tucked Hannah's hair behind her ears. "Just look how far you've come. You trained a dog. You learned to surf. A million people want to be your friend. The other dog owners in your class are trying really hard to help you. And you helped Mrs. Gilly so much. I know it's tough right now, but try not to see only the bad stuff. You have to see the good, too."

"What good?" Hannah sniffled. "Poppy's still missing."

"Yes, Poppy is still out there," her mom said. "But we'll find her. And it will be because of you. We all saw it at the obedience test yesterday—you have an amazing way of guiding her and caring for her, and you two have a very special bond. You saw the good in Poppy, and it made all the difference in the world for her. And now it'll make all the difference in bringing her home. You'll see."

Her dad came over and joined the hug. "We'll find her," he promised.

For the first time since they'd moved to California, Hannah felt warm and safe, sandwiched between her parents. And yet, though she wanted to believe them, with each minute that passed, it was hard not to worry more.

★ CHAPTER 24 ★

The next morning, Hannah sat in the Adirondack chair on the porch, hugging her knees to her chest. Jess, Marcy, and her mom were out combing the streets for Poppy. Hannah had her phone and a book beside her, but she couldn't concentrate. She just kept scanning the street. Everyone had told her she should wait at home while the search continued, in case Poppy came back on her own. She desperately wanted to be out pounding the pavement instead of being stuck in one place, but she knew they were right. Someone had to be there if Poppy came back.

No, *when* Poppy came back. Hannah thought about what her mom had said the day before. She had to try to stay positive, for Poppy's sake. She had made a difference —Poppy had been happy and loved and safe, and Hannah knew that would give the dog a reason to want to come home.

Yet it was hard to sit still.

Mrs. Gilly made her way across the front yard and up the walkway. She'd traded her walker for a cane, and she was getting around more easily. But she still moved slowly and carefully. When she reached the edge of the porch, Hannah jumped up to help her up the stairs and into a chair.

Mrs. Gilly sat, catching her breath. Hannah picked at the hem of her shirt. She still couldn't look Mrs. Gilly in the eye. She'd never felt so guilty in her life. As much as her world had turned gray and senseless without Poppy, she could only imagine what it was like for Mrs. Gilly, who lived alone and had to look at the dog's toys and bowls and the chewed-up spot on the couch every day.

"I'm so sorry," Hannah said. "I wish I'd done a better job training Poppy. All I wanted was for you to be able to keep her."

Mrs. Gilly shook her head. "Oh, Hannah. Don't be so hard on yourself. You made Poppy into the best dog she could be."

"But it's my fault that she's missing!" Hannah's stomach clenched every time she replayed the moment Poppy slipped out of her collar. She should have seen how nervous Poppy was and reassured her. She should have kept her closer.

"It could have happened to anyone." Mrs. Gilly patted Hannah's hand. They sat in silence for a minute, watching the street. "I just want my dog to come home," Mrs. Gilly said quietly.

"Me too," Hannah said. "I miss her."

"I miss her smile." Mrs. Gilly smiled sadly.

"I miss the way she bounced when she was excited," Hannah said.

"I miss the way she curled up by my feet when I read and rested her head on my slippers," Mrs. Gilly said.

Hannah nodded. The memories hurt and soothed her at the same time. She imagined Mrs. Gilly felt the same way. Poppy was such a happy dog, she made everyone around her happy—but that just made her absence all the more painful.

★　★　★

After Mrs. Gilly left, Hannah was alone again on the porch when she saw Sophia coming around the corner, taking Louie for a walk. When she noticed Hannah out on the porch, Sophia ducked her head and started to cross the street, Louie scrambling to keep up. But then she stopped, stood still for a moment as if deciding what to do, and crossed back to Hannah's house.

Louie bounded up the porch steps, his tail wagging as he sniffed around and looked for Poppy. "She's not here," Hannah said, stroking his soft fur. Seeing him was a hard reminder of what—or who—was missing, but petting him also comforted her. He leaned against her legs.

"So, um, school starts soon," Sophia said. "Are you taking the bus?"

"I think so," Hannah said. School was the furthest thing from her mind, but she was pretty sure her parents wouldn't have time to drive her. She didn't even care whether riding the bus was considered cool or not at Deerwood Middle School.

"Me too. We'll be on the same bus." Sophia wrapped and unwrapped Louie's leash around her hand. She shifted on her feet, as if she was unsure what to do with herself. Hannah couldn't think of anything to say. She felt like she was watching the whole awkward conversation from far away.

"Have you heard from Althea?" Sophia asked.

Hannah nodded. Althea had been texting her almost every hour for Poppy updates and to repeat to Hannah that it wasn't her fault. Linnea had been doing the same. But she figured Sophia didn't want to hear about that. "Althea starts school this week," Hannah said.

"I'm glad our summer isn't over yet."

"Yeah," Hannah agreed, though she thought it might as well be. It wasn't like she would be hanging out at the beach or having fun with the dog. The only good thing was that she wouldn't be stuck in a classroom when she needed to be here, waiting for Poppy.

Sophia gestured at Louie, who had rolled onto his back

and was pawing Hannah's leg for a belly rub. "Is this okay?" Sophia asked.

Something about her question loosened the knot in Hannah's chest and relieved the awkwardness between them just a little bit. It brought Hannah back into the moment.

"Yeah." Hannah sniffled, holding back tears. "Louie's a sweet puppy. And I'm really sorry about the cake—I mean, the second cake. Well, the first one, too."

"I saw what happened at graduation," Sophia said in a rush. "It wasn't Poppy's fault. Trixie jumped on that table all on her own. It was just a coincidence about the cake— Poppy is a really good dog. I just . . . overreacted . . . and I'm sorry too."

Hannah looked up at her, surprised and overwhelmed by Sophia's words.

"We've been trying to look for her—Jackie, Taylor, and me. We even went back to the park again. I wish we'd found her." Sophia fiddled with Louie's leash. "Anyway, I know it's another week away, but I hope you'll sit with us at school."

Hannah swallowed the lump in her throat. After everything they'd been through, she wasn't sure what to say. She'd been so hurt and confused by the way Sophia had treated her all summer, but the truth was, Sophia seemed to genuinely care about Poppy.

And Hannah would really be happy if she didn't have to start the school year all alone.

Sophia filled the silence with words Hannah never expected to hear. "I'm sorry I was mean when you first got here. You seemed so smart and cool, and then Jackie and Taylor really liked you. I was worried you were going to take away my friends. I know I wasn't nice, but—I don't know . . . It's not an excuse, but maybe it's just easier to be mean than to let new people in."

"I thought you were being mean to me because of my birthmark," Hannah confessed before she could stop herself.

"I wouldn't do that," Sophia said a little too quickly.

"A lot of people do."

"That's terrible." Sophia's gaze flitted to Hannah's cheek for a split second, then back to her eyes. "I mean, I didn't know what to do at first. I didn't know if I should look at it or not, and I didn't want to stare, but then I felt like I wasn't looking at you. I just kind of freaked out. And then I felt bad because I knew I was being rude and figured you probably hated me for it."

"I didn't hate you," Hannah said. "I just wanted you to give me a chance."

"Honestly, I was being inconsiderate, and I'm so, so sorry." Sophia shrugged, embarrassed. "It's just one part of you. I don't even notice it anymore."

"It happens a lot," Hannah said. "People assume things about me or act like they might catch it if they get too close. But I'm glad you got over it."

"It's just a birthmark," Sophia said. "People shouldn't care about it. And I'm glad you're my friend."

"Me too." Hannah managed a small smile.

Sophia smiled back shyly. "Anyway, I hope you find Poppy soon."

"Thanks." Hannah curled up in the big chair as Sophia and Louie walked back down the street. Poppy managed to bring people together even when she wasn't there. Hannah was glad she and Sophia were friends now, but as long as Poppy was gone, there would always be a giant, aching puppy-shaped hole in her heart.

★ CHAPTER 25 ★

The doorbell rang the next morning, summoning Hannah out of bed. She answered the door in her pajamas to find Jackie and Taylor standing on her porch. She rubbed the sleep out of her eyes, blinking in the bright sunlight. It was like déjà vu of that first morning Althea came to her door. Why were they at her house? And where was Sophia? What was going on?

"You need to come surfing," Taylor said.

"The waves are amazing," Jackie added.

"Seriously perfect," Taylor said, bouncing impatiently on her toes. "Come with us right now."

Jackie's eyes were wide and pleading.

Hannah noticed that their hair was wet and sand clung to their flip-flops. They'd already been at the beach, but they'd come all the way back to get her.

Hannah hesitated. She hadn't felt like having fun since

Poppy ran off. But she remembered Mrs. Gilly saying she shouldn't be so hard on herself. And she thought about everything Sophia had said about the girls really wanting to be friends with her. School was starting in just a few days. Hannah was scared to open herself up and risk getting hurt again, but maybe she should give Jackie and Taylor more of a chance.

Jackie tugged Hannah's arm. "Come on. We need you to surf with us right now!"

"Okay," she said. "Let me just get changed."

"Hurry!" Taylor said.

Hannah got into her bathing suit and rash guard as quickly as she could, and Jackie and Taylor practically dragged her out the door. She didn't even get a chance to grab her beach bag, because the girls didn't want to wait. They promised they had extra towels and sunscreen. Hannah had to jog to keep up with them as they hurried back to the beach. She tried to imagine what the waves must be like to get them so excited. Or maybe they were just being nice and trying extra hard to make her feel better.

When they got to the beach, Hannah spotted Sophia waiting for them. Sophia kept glancing nervously over her shoulder toward the surfboard rental hut. Something didn't feel right, and Hannah slowed down as they got closer.

"What's going on?" Hannah asked. Without answering, Sophia took one wide step to her left, revealing one of the rental surfboards that had been knocked over and lay flat in the sand. A brown and white dog lay on top of the board with her big, square head on her paws.

The dog had a familiar spot on her face—one that looked just like a birthmark.

"Poppy!" Hannah shouted. At the sound of Hannah's voice, Poppy raised her head and thumped her tail against the board. When she saw Hannah, Poppy jumped up and raced across the sand. Hannah dropped to her knees and threw her arms around the dog, and Poppy gave her a million licks and kisses.

Poppy danced around so much that she kicked sand up everywhere. The dog whimpered and snorted, as if she were apologizing for running off.

"It's okay," Hannah said. "But promise me you won't ever disappear like that again!"

"She was here when we got here early this morning," Sophia said. "The guy at the rental hut said he thinks she spent the night on the beach. We would've brought her home right away, but we couldn't get her to move. I've never seen her look so sad."

"We tried dog treats and bacon. We even tried to get her in the water, but she didn't want any of it," Taylor said.

"She let us pet her," Jackie added. "But she wouldn't come with us."

"She was waiting for you," Sophia said.

Hannah sat down in the sand and Poppy crawled onto her lap, pressing close against her. Hannah wrapped her in a tight hug. After a moment the dog finally started to calm down, safe in the arms of the person she trusted the most.

"I missed you, too," Hannah whispered into Poppy's soft neck. Poppy smelled like ocean and sunlight. She seemed a little skinny, and she definitely needed a good bath. Hannah wondered where she'd been — and what she had gone through to find her way back. Hannah would never know, but maybe, in the end, it didn't matter. Poppy was home.

Hannah managed to work her phone out of her pocket and called her house. Her dad answered, sounding worried. "Are you okay?"

It was hard to talk with Poppy trying to lick her face.

"Hannah? Are you there?" her dad asked.

"Yes! I'm here," Hannah managed. "And so is Poppy!"

"You found her? Hannah found Poppy!"

Hannah's mom picked up the phone. One of the twins was squealing in the background. "You have Poppy? Oh, I'm so relieved. What happened? Where are you?"

"I can't believe it," Hannah said. "I got here, and there

she was. I should've known she'd wind up here. This is our spot."

Hannah was so excited, she was having a hard time making any sense.

"Where?" her mom asked.

"The beach!" Hannah shouted.

"Stay there," her mom said. "Your dad went next door to tell Mrs. Gilly. We're on our way."

Hannah disconnected and let her phone fall to the sand so she could fold Poppy into a hug again. But Poppy wouldn't settle down—she was too busy bursting with excitement.

"What are we going to do with all your energy?" Hannah said, laughing as Poppy sprang and hopped around her, her whole body vibrating with happiness.

"Want to use my board?" Sophia offered. "Poppy looks like she needs to ride some waves."

"We'd love to!" Hannah said. She hoped the dog would calm down a little before her parents showed up with Mrs. Gilly. She didn't want Poppy to knock Mrs. Gilly over now! But mostly, Hannah accepted the board from Sophia because she wanted nothing more than to be out on the waves with her dog. She'd missed Poppy so much—she didn't want to miss out on another second of fun together.

"What do you think, Poppy? Want to surf?"

Poppy barked and bounced on her front paws. Hannah jogged toward the water with the board under her arm, trying not to trip over Poppy as the dog zigzagged back and forth in front of her. Whatever Poppy had been through, she was still her same joyful self, ready for anything.

As soon as the board was in the water, Poppy hopped onto it. Hannah climbed on behind her and paddled out to the waves. When they got far enough out, Hannah sat up to wait for a good swell. As they bobbed in the water, she ran her fingers through the wet fur on Poppy's back and let out a sigh of such contentment, such relief, that Poppy looked back over her shoulder at Hannah.

Then the perfect wave rolled toward them. "Ready, girl?" Hannah turned the board and started paddling. Poppy stood in anticipation. Instead of sliding off the board to let Poppy ride, Hannah stayed with her dog, and Poppy found her footing as the wave lifted them. Hannah paddled hard to get them in front of the crest, and at the right moment she popped onto her feet.

The board wobbled beneath them. For a second, Hannah thought she'd tumble off the back or that Poppy would jump off into the water. But she relaxed her knees, Poppy shifted her stance, and they regained their balance. As the wave carried them toward shore, she and Poppy were perfectly in sync—just as they had been before. Poppy's tongue was out and her smile was huge. As they sliced through the water and the ocean breeze swept back her hair, Hannah thought her own grin might be just as big.

Hannah was exactly where she was supposed to be.

They hopped off the board into the shallow water at the same time, Poppy splashing around as Sophia, Jackie, and Taylor ran up to them.

Taylor held up her palm for a high-five. "That was the coolest thing I've ever seen!" she said.

Sophia turned her phone toward Hannah and hit play on the video, saying, "Check it out." Hannah watched as she and Poppy rode the wave like pros. Offscreen, cheering drowned out the sound of the ocean.

"You and Poppy look like you've been surfing together your whole life," Sophia said. "Like you belong together on that board."

Hannah couldn't stop smiling. She finally felt like she *did* belong. She scooped up the board and pointed it back toward the waves. "Ready to go again?" she asked Poppy.

Poppy let out a happy bark and traipsed after Hannah into the ocean.

★ CHAPTER 26 ★

Hannah snapped a picture of herself in the mirror. She was wearing her favorite jeans and a sky blue T-shirt she'd bought at the surf shop on the boardwalk. Her hair was loose, the color lighter from all the time she'd spent in the sun. She sent the picture off to Althea and Linnea.

Both friends texted back within seconds.

Althea sent her two thumbs-up emojis. *Looking good!*

Perfect! Linnea wrote. *Good luck today!*

Hannah wasn't nervous at all about the first day of school. She already felt lucky to have two best friends who lived in totally different parts of the country. Maybe someday they'd both visit at the same time and get to meet each other. And even if all the other kids in her class stared at the new girl with the birthmark, she knew that Sophia, Jackie, and Taylor would have her back.

Hannah's mom was getting the twins dressed while her dad was in charge of getting her and Jenny off to school. He was already toasting a bagel for Jenny when Hannah reached the kitchen. "What can I make you for your first day?" he asked.

"Nothing." Hannah grabbed a banana and a breakfast bar off the counter. "I have to go!"

"Tell Poppy I say hi!" Jenny called after her.

On the way out the front door, Hannah stopped to get a dog treat. She ran next door, where Mrs. Gilly and Poppy were waiting on their porch.

Poppy sat politely by Mrs. Gilly's side. Her tail began swishing back and forth when she saw Hannah.

"Be good," Hannah said as she gave Poppy the dog treat. "I promise I'll come play with you after school."

"You'll do great," Mrs. Gilly said. "I'm sure you'll make lots of friends."

"I know," Hannah replied. She rubbed Poppy's ears. "I already have."

Mrs. Gilly smiled. "Here comes the bus."

The school bus pulled up in front of Hannah's house. Hannah gave Poppy a quick kiss on the brown patch of fur on her face. She ran to catch the bus, her bag bouncing against her back.

When she climbed onboard, it was full of unfamiliar faces. Hannah thought she recognized a few from the beach, but she didn't know their names. Then she spotted Sophia.

"Hey, Hannah!" Sophia waved at her. "I saved a seat for you."

Hannah slid in beside her friend. The two girls in the row in front of them twisted around to talk to Sophia. The girls across the aisle leaned in too. Hannah felt everyone's eyes on her. She glanced out the window and saw Mrs. Gilly waving goodbye as she and Poppy watched the bus pull away.

"This is my new friend, Hannah," Sophia said. "She just moved here from Michigan. She's supercool and is already a great surfer. We spent almost the whole summer at the beach together." Sophia grinned at her. "And she's besties with a pretty cool dog, too."

"I love dogs! What kind?" asked one of the girls in front of them.

"Can we see a picture?" her seatmate chimed in.

"Sure." Hannah unzipped her backpack and took out her phone. Her screen saver was a picture of Poppy on the surf-board. She held out her phone to the girls. "She's a pit bull, and she's the best."

Hannah watched as they passed the phone back and forth, exclaiming how cute Poppy was.

"She really surfs," Sophia said. She pulled up the videos of Poppy catching a wave.

"No way!" One of the girls watched the screen with wide eyes. "How did you get her to do that?"

Hannah shrugged. "Poppy's a natural. She practically taught me how to surf."

"She really trusts you," Sophia said. "I don't think a dog would surf with someone they didn't truly love."

Hannah warmed at the compliment. She and Poppy did have a special bond.

"You should take her to one of those surf dog competitions," a girl across the aisle said.

"There are competitions?" Hannah asked.

"They're the cutest thing ever," the girl said. "And Poppy could totally win."

"Maybe I will." Hannah settled into her seat while the girls made plans to take their own dogs to the beach that weekend. They all wanted her and Poppy to teach their dogs to surf.

Hannah watched her new classmates chattering and laughing and realized how lucky she was. She had been so upset when her parents told her they were moving across the country—and ripping her from her old life in Michigan. She'd been miserable when they first got to California. But then she met Poppy, and everything changed in ways she never could have imagined.

How could Hannah ever have guessed that she'd be surrounded by new friends on her first day of school, with everyone talking about her surfing dog. She still missed her old friends, but her new life in California was full of adventure and exciting possibilities. She smiled, tucking her hair behind her ears, ready to take on the world.

★ ALL ABOUT THE PIT BULL ★

★ The pit bull is actually not a breed of dog, but is a collection of breeds that were mixed together over the course of centuries until they could no longer be identified separately. Because there are such big differences in the bloodlines of pit bulls, they don't have only one body type. Some are petite, weighing as little as forty pounds. Others are broad chested, with sturdy shoulders, and can reach as much as eighty pounds.

★ Pit bulls are known for being intelligent, energetic, and determined dogs who are extremely loyal to the people they love. They are playful but also very responsive to training.

★ Pit bulls pass annual temperament tests (done on many common breeds of dogs) with a pleasant and positive temperament 86.4 percent of the time. That's better than many popular breeds such as golden retrievers and beagles!

★ Pit bulls have one of the best smiles in the canine world. They are known for pulling their lips back in a happy expression that resembles a human smile.

★ Pit bulls were once bred to be hunting and fighting dogs, and many have been used in illegal dogfighting rings. Because of this history, the pit bull sometimes has a negative reputation. Many people believe that all pit bulls are dangerous and aggressive. This is not true, but like any dog, the pit bull does need proper training and socialization, or time spent with people and other dogs, in order to learn to behave properly.

★ Because they have a negative reputation, pit bulls end up in rescues and animal shelters more often than almost any other breed. In fact, nearly 40 percent of dogs in US shelters are labeled pit bulls. Unfortunately, because of their bad reputation—and laws in some places making it illegal to own a pit bull—these dogs have a much harder time finding homes.

★ For a long time, people have said that pit bulls have locking jaws that cannot be opened once they bite. This is not true, although, like many breeds, pit bulls do have a very strong bite.

★ Pit bulls have a long history in America. The first ones are said to have come from England with the first colonial settlers. In 1993, Weela, a California pit bull, rescued thirty-two people, twenty-nine dogs, three horses, and one cat during a severe and widespread flood.

A huge variety of both purebred and mixed-breed dogs are available for adoption from your local pet rescue. It is important to think carefully about how your family will care for and interact with a rescue dog, so you can choose a breed that's just right for your household. If you have questions about whether a certain type of dog is right for you, contact a local veterinarian or your local rescue, or do a thorough Internet search to find the dog that would fit best with your family. This helps keep more dogs from returning to shelters and will help you enjoy a lifetime of happiness with your pet.

★ ACKNOWLEDGMENTS ★

Behind every book is an amazing group of people . . . and in this case, fellow dog lovers. Thank you to Emilia Rhodes, Catherine Onder, and the sales, marketing, publicity, and design teams at HMH. Many thanks to Les Morgenstein, Josh Bank, Sara Shandler, Romy Golan, and Laura Barbiea at Alloy Entertainment. And endless gratitude to Robin Straus, Katelyn Hales, Stephanie Feldstein, and my book partner in crime, Hayley Wagreich.

There will never be enough ways to say thank you to Brian, the goons, Virginia Wing, Kunsang Bhuti, Tenzin Dekyi, and Vida, the best/worst dog ever, but I'll keep trying.

Turn the page for a preview of

AMERICAN DOG

★ BRAVE ★

#1 New York Times Bestselling Author JENNIFER LI SHOTZ

★ CHAPTER 1 ★

"How about these?" Dylan held out a plastic packet of multicolored water balloons.

Jaxon, his best friend since forever, took the pack from Dylan's hand and held it up for inspection. "Perfect," he declared. "Just the right size for a good soaking."

The boys were gearing up for their last epic water balloon fight of the season. School had started for the year, but it was still hot enough in Texas for a full-scale battle—and Dylan and Jaxon were an unstoppable team. Their signature move was to ambush their friends from two sides at once—and they'd never lost. Not once.

Jaxon tossed the package back to Dylan, who caught it in midair.

Dylan grabbed four more water balloon packs from the rack and headed for the register.

"When are we doing this?" Dylan asked. "Tomorrow?"

"If you can handle it!" Jaxon punched him on the shoulder and Dylan winced.

"You're going to regret that!" Dylan chased Jaxon to the front of the store, where the cashier eyed them sternly.

The boys slowed to a walk. Dylan cleared his throat and dumped a handful of change on the counter. Jaxon's long brown hair flopped into his eyes as he looked down and turned his jeans pockets inside out to grab every last coin. Together they had just enough, even if Dylan was contributing more of his allowance than Jaxon was.

"I'll take those." Dylan grabbed the shopping bag from Jaxon as they walked out of the store. He hopped on his bike, ready to head for home. "I'll text you later to make a plan of attack. I have some ideas for a new strategy."

"Hey, Dyl, actually, I had an idea too." Jaxon rubbed his chin thoughtfully, like he had thought of something brilliant. "What if we ditch the fight and do something else entirely?"

Dylan shot Jaxon a skeptical look, to be sure his friend wasn't just messing with him. The showdown was tradition. Why wouldn't Jaxon want to play—or win—anymore? "What are you talking about?" Dylan asked doubtfully.

"I'm just saying, maybe now that we're in sixth grade, having a water balloon fight every weekend is for little kids." Jaxon shrugged like it was no big deal.

Dylan couldn't believe it—Jaxon was serious. "I mean . . . I guess, maybe?" Dylan tried not to sound disappointed. If Jaxon suddenly thought the whole thing was babyish, he didn't want to admit that he was looking forward to it.

Since kindergarten, Dylan and Jaxon had always been like two sides of the same coin. They had played on the same soccer teams and gone to the same swimming classes. They had even looked alike until recently, when Dylan had his dark brown hair buzzed down to the usual crew cut to match his dad's military cut, while Jaxon had let his hair grow out.

But Dylan had to admit that it wasn't just their hair that had changed recently. Dylan had also noticed that at school, the other guys had started to treat Jaxon a little differently. It was like he and Jaxon and their friends had always been a pack—equals—but now Jaxon had moved to the front of it, and the guys would do anything he told them to. Dylan had started to feel less like Jaxon's friend and more like his follower. It seemed to Dylan that Jaxon had noticed it too—and kind of liked it.

"Come on, Dyl—don't you ever get . . . I don't know . . . tired of doing the same stuff all the time?"

The question took Dylan by surprise. "Uh . . . no. I mean, sometimes?" He felt something squirm in his stomach—like somehow Jaxon was reading his mind. He did get tired of some stuff, but not the water balloon fights. "I just think we should do something *really* different this time," Jaxon said. "We're twelve. Maybe we should do something . . . I don't know . . . cooler."

Jaxon's words stung, but Dylan did his best not to let it show. He couldn't say Jaxon's suggestion was coming out of nowhere. With his new status, Jaxon had been pushing boundaries lately, as Dylan's mom would call it—asking Dylan to stay out late, skipping his homework, and thinking up elaborate pranks. Dylan liked having fun, and Jaxon always acted like whatever he had in mind was going to be the *most* fun thing ever. And if Dylan or one of the other guys hesitated, Jaxon was quick to tease them in front of everyone else.

So Dylan had been telling himself to just go along with whatever Jaxon suggested, even when he wasn't so sure it was such a good idea. *What's the worst that can happen?* he'd recently found himself wondering more often than he'd care to admit.

"Like what?" Dylan asked, trying to sound cool himself.

Jaxon shrugged and jumped onto his bike. "Let me think . . ." A strange look crossed his face that Dylan had never seen before. There was a glint in his eye and a smirk on his lips—and it made Dylan instantly uncomfortable.

"Um, why are you looking at me like that?" Dylan asked, not entirely sure he wanted to know the answer.

"You know that video I sent you? Of the guy with the hose?"

Dylan nodded, hoping Jaxon wouldn't notice that he was just playing along. He didn't remember that video because he hadn't watched it — or most of the others Jaxon and their other friends had sent in the last few days. He'd meant to, and even held his finger above the play arrow a couple of times. But he just hadn't done it. Lately, while Jaxon and their other friends were high-fiving and fist-bumping and *hey-bro*-ing about things Dylan usually cared about, he found himself tuning out. What so-and-so posted on Instagram. The latest Nintendo news. A viral YouTube video. Sometimes Dylan thought it just seemed . . . boring.

"Yeah, sure. That one was crazy," Dylan said.

Jaxon broke out into a full grin. "So what if we copied that video, but instead of using a hose, we throw water balloons at the cars?"

This time, Dylan's stomach did a full churning somersault. "You want to throw water balloons . . . at cars? Isn't that . . . I mean, that's not . . . Is that a good idea?"

Jaxon's eyes bulged out of his head. "A good idea? It's a great idea!"

Dylan just stared back at him, unsure what to say. It was a terrible idea—a dangerous idea. This time, Jaxon was going too far.

"Come on, Dyl—I thought you'd be up for a little adventure." Jaxon mouthed *boom!* and mimed a water balloon exploding with his hands. He was getting excited now.

Dylan was quiet as he thought it over. He didn't want to say yes, but he really didn't know how to say no.

"Dude!" Jaxon laughed. "What is going on with you? What have you done with my best friend?"

"Nothing!" Dylan forced himself to smile.

"Good. Because I don't want to tell anyone else until after we do it. It'll be so much crazier if we surprise the guys with our own video."

Something about the look in Jaxon's eye told Dylan that he wasn't going to take no for an answer, even if Dylan tried to get out of it.

"Tomorrow. We're doing this," Jaxon said.

"Okay, fine, we're doing this."

Before Jaxon could question his enthusiasm, Dylan's phone buzzed in his back pocket. Secretly relieved at the interruption, he checked the alert reminding him to get home. He had promised his mom he'd do his chores and get a head start on his homework, but if he didn't leave soon, he was going to be late.

"I . . . um . . . I'll see you tomorrow," Dylan said.

Jaxon zoomed past Dylan with a cackle and grabbed the bag of water balloons out of his hand. "It's gonna be awesome, Dyl!" he shouted over his shoulder, now in the lead.

"Yeah," Dylan muttered to himself, pedaling slowly after his friend. "Awesome. Right."

★ CHAPTER 2 ★

The wind whipped against Dylan's face as he raced his bike down the street. He'd left Jaxon at the turnoff to his street and had to hurry home if he had any hope of beating his mom. He swerved around a tree branch lying at an angle in the road—a remnant of the hurricane that had pounded the city a couple of weeks earlier.

Not that Dylan needed any reminders. The memory of the hurricane was burned into his brain forever: the wind as loud as a speeding train, trees snapping like twigs and slamming into buildings, windows exploding like they'd been dynamited. It had been a terrifying few hours. He and his mom had spent the entire night lying awake in their bathtub, listening to the destruction outside and hoping the walls around them would withstand the force of the storm.

The city had hauled away most of the big wreckage, but there were still pockets of splintered plywood and wet debris scattered on the streets. The shock from the storm lingered along with the mess, but people had jumped into action to try to help one another through it. Neighbors had banded together to carry bucket after bucket of water from flooded living rooms. They had cleaned up yards and hammered boards over the gaping holes in the sides of their houses. People from the block had been especially helpful to Dylan and his mom because his dad was a soldier deployed in the Middle East.

Countless families had been forced to move out of their mangled homes, and it seemed like a lot of them might not ever come back. Dylan knew he and his mom had been lucky. Except for a few patches of roof that had been sheared right off, and a giant hole in the exterior wall by the front door, their house had fared pretty well.

Dylan sped up, swerving toward the sidewalk when he saw that the street ahead was clogged with traffic. He scooted back on the seat, shifting his weight until he was about to tip over, then yanked up on the handlebars at just the right second. He popped a half wheelie over the curb and whizzed by a woman carrying a bag of groceries to her car.

"Hey!" she yelled.

"Sorry!" Dylan shouted behind him. He kept going, reminding himself to slow down around pedestrians.

As Dylan made his way down the street, a delicious smell wafted toward him. He would know that scent anywhere: Tio Suerte tacos, voted best tacos in San Antonio three years running. They'd been closed since the hurricane, and Dylan's stomach rumbled at the thought of them finally being reopened. He could practically taste the beef taco already.

One little detour couldn't hurt.

He pulled a hard left and slammed on his handlebar brakes, skidding to a stop on the loose gravel in the Tio Suerte parking lot. Just as he dropped his bike to the ground, Dylan heard a man shout in the alley behind the restaurant.

"Get out of here, you dirty little rat!"

Dylan stuck his head around the side of the building and peeked down the alley. An old man in an apron waved a fist in the air—but it wasn't a rat he was chasing—it was a dirty gray dog. The cook stomped his foot on the asphalt, and the dog whimpered and scuttled backwards into the corner by the dumpster, his ears back and down and his tail tucked between his legs. The chef was angry—really angry —and Dylan could tell that the dog was scared.

The cook grabbed a broom and whacked the handle hard against the side of the metal dumpster, which let out a terrifying rumble. The dog flinched at the loud noise. The man was trying to scare the dog away, but the pup was so petrified that it was having the opposite effect.

"Get out of here!" the cook shouted. *"¡Lágate!"*

The dog hunkered down, shaking. Dylan had recently seen a few other strays wandering the city. He wondered if there were more of them because of the hurricane. But there was something about this dog that caught Dylan's eye—it seemed so scared and sad. Did this pup have a family?

Dylan suddenly felt protective of the poor dog, who had probably just been following the mouth-watering aroma of the tacos, like he had.

"I think he's hungry," Dylan called to the cook.

The man shot him an irritated look. "Every day he's hungry. The little monster won't leave."

Dylan studied the animal more closely. The dog looked from him to the cook and back again with big, round, frightened eyes—eyes that were a surprisingly intense amber color. There was no way this dog had a home, Dylan thought. His ribs were showing under his fur, and he was filthy—his coat was matted and stiff. He wasn't wearing a collar or tags. And why would he stick around an alley getting yelled at if he had somewhere else to be? He had to be a stray.

"How long has he been hanging around?" Dylan asked, getting closer.

"He's been here for at least a week," the chef replied. "I've called animal control a hundred times, but this dog is too fast. They can't catch him." As the cook spoke, he took a step forward and tried to grab the dog. But the pup really was quick—he disappeared under the dumpster as the cook's fingers snatched at nothing but air.

The cook waved the broom handle one last time, then went inside, slamming the kitchen door behind him.

The second the man was gone, the dog popped his nose out and sniffed at the air, then scanned the alley. When he saw that the coast was clear, he crept out from under the dumpster and looked up at Dylan.

"You okay, boy?" Dylan asked, speaking softly. He didn't want to scare the dog more.

The dog gave a nervous wag of his tail and gazed at Dylan with a sweet but desperate look in his eye.

Dylan and the dog stared at each other while Dylan's mind buzzed.

Clearly this dog was starving. He couldn't just leave it here, could he? That's not the type of thing his parents had raised him to do—to leave someone in trouble. And this dog was definitely in trouble.

Don't miss these heartwarming and adventurous tales of rescue dogs in the **AMERICAN DOG** series by **JENNIFER LI SHOTZ**.

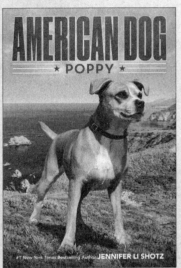

JENNIFER LI SHOTZ is the author of *Max: Best Friend. Hero. Marine* and the Hero and Scout series, about brave dogs and their humans. Jen was a cat person until she and her family adopted a sweet, stubborn, adorable rescue pup, who occasionally lets Jen sit on the couch. Jen lives with her family in Brooklyn, loves chocolate chip cookies with very few chips, and still secretly loves cats. Please don't tell the dog. For the occasional tweet, follow her @jenshotz.